WASHINGTON SPIES

PHYLLIS BOWDEN BOOK 3

SJ SLAGLE

ROUGH EDGES PRESS

Washington Spies
Paperback Edition
© Copyright 2022 SJ Slagle

Rough Edges Press
An Imprint of Wolfpack Publishing
5130 S. Fort Apache Rd. 215-380
Las Vegas, NV 89148

roughedgespress.com

Paperback ISBN 978-1-68549-066-9
LCCN 2022930240

WASHINGTON SPIES

PROLOGUE

THE CAPTURE

As she stared at the decrepit building, Phyllis Bowden's clammy hands slipped off the steering wheel. Warm liquid oozed from her body onto the seat. The bleeding hadn't stopped.

Rough-looking men, secret police probably, rushed in the front door of the building at the same time her target and his pregnant wife stumbled onto the rickety fire escape on the third floor.

Phyllis held her breath, watching him help her from one landing to another, rushing the best he could. The third-floor landing shivered with the unexpected weight. The second-floor landing swayed precariously, making Phyllis light-headed with breathless anticipation. She was able to suck in some air when the man maneuvered the woman to the ground level. Phyllis inched her car along the icy street, narrowly missing another car trying to pass her. A horn blared unwanted attention and she hissed a curse.

Much was riding on this defection. If she couldn't bring in the target, his life and his wife's, plus that of their unborn child, would be worth nothing. They would be shot for sure.

Her job was at stake. Even though higher-ups on the food chain had chosen her for this assignment, she was still trying to prove herself to a boss who didn't think much of her abilities as an agent.

Most important of all, the atomic spy they had been chasing would escape justice. This man was as elusive as he was dangerous. Just when the agency thought they had him cornered, he'd slip out of their net. Just when a witness to his treason was found, he or she disappeared nearly as quickly as they had come.

More liquid trickled down her leg.

Parked at the curb by the old tavern, Phyllis kept her focus on the two people slipping toward her. Their breaths were frosty in the chilly air. The man glanced at Phyllis. She read desperation and fear in his eyes. He was doubtful this would work out, that much was obvious. If so, why had he pursued this course of action? No one had talked him into this. He'd come to them.

Snow fell heavily, caking their boots, making movement sluggish. The landscape would soon be covered. Phyllis opened the passenger door. He reached her at the same time.

"Get in. We've got to go." Glancing up, she saw men stepping onto the third-floor landing. Their dark looks took in the scene with a glance.

"Come on, honey. It's not far now," he told his wife.

She didn't bother responding. With hands caressing her bloated belly, the woman panted from exertion. It took the two of them to heave her into the front passenger seat, her heavy load nearly reaching the dashboard of the tiny car. The man slipped into the back.

Phyllis' tires left deep ruts in the snowy street. Slush covered her car's wiper blades rendering her vision bleary. No matter. Weaving around slower traffic, she kept her car pointed north. North to the safe house. Even with her precious cargo, she pushed the little Chevy faster than she should have. A pedestrian appeared out of nowhere, walking into her hazy line of sight.

She stomped the brakes. The woman braced her hands against the dash to prevent being thrown forward. Phyllis automatically threw a hand over to protect her.

"You okay?" she asked.

"Fine," she puffed. "Just keep going."

A sharp pain stabbed Phyllis' abdomen causing her to groan aloud.

Recklessly, Phyllis careened her car forward into traffic. With an eye on her rearview mirror, she could see two black sedans weaving around cars trying to catch up. She cursed the rental agency for only having the one compact car left in the lot, when she needed something with more get-up-and-go. Also, she wasn't particularly smooth with the stick transmission and vainly wished she'd listened more to Joe's patient instructions.

Grinding another gear, Phyllis sped down the street toward her destination. With the cars in pursuit closing in, she ran a red light. A traffic policeman blew his shrill whistle noisily at her. Unable to stop Phyllis, the policeman was able to halt one black sedan from crossing after her. He pointed to the side of road, effectively taking one car out of the race.

By the time the second car was able to cross the

intersection, Phyllis was well ahead, coming within sight of her destination. She kept her head down, one hand cradling her stomach and her foot on the accelerator.

The safe house was within sight.

ONE

PHYLLIS

If she hurried, Phyllis Bowden had just enough time for a quick sandwich at the corner drugstore. Tuna on white bread would hold her until dinner. She'd eaten here nearly every workday for the year she'd been in Washington, D.C. The small drugstore was close, served good food and fast. She could be in and out in twenty minutes, leaving the bulk of her lunch hour for the old bookstore down the block.

She paid her check and left a good tip for Flo, the smiling waitress with the bouffant hairdo who had served her the past six months. Flo's husband sold Kirby vacuum cleaners door-to-door and wasn't very good at it. Flo worked at the drugstore to make ends meet, but according to her, they did all right.

The war was over and doing all right was pretty much the song everyone was singing. Since Phyllis had been in London at the end of the war and then in Oslo, Norway the year after that, she was ready to settle in her hometown and live her life.

With Joe.

Joe Schneider. Just thinking about her dear husband brought a smile to her face. They'd met in London with the bombs still dropping. After that, he was nearly killed on assignment in Bucharest. They married on board ship on the way back to the States, not daring to waste a moment longer.

Leaving the drugstore, she pulled out a compact from her purse. Sparkling brown eyes looked back at her in the small mirror. She patted her shiny nose, gave her no-nonsense hairdo the once over. Smoothing down curly hair, the color of creamy milk chocolate, was all she needed to do. Tucking the compact away, she nearly bounced down the street. Life was a bed of roses.

A romance writer could have imagined the old bookstore. Two enormous windows flanked the open door, revealing books lining the walls within and gathered on shelves like butterflies ready to launch.

A wooden bench sat by the door, accompanied by a huge urn filled with yellow chrysanthemums. A small bookshelf on the other side of the door was being picked over by a customer taking his time. More urns captured Phyllis' attention with pink and red roses drenching her with their heavenly scent. The season for flowers was nearly over, making the aroma more precious.

She wandered around the store, perusing titles she wanted to buy, but there were too many to choose from. The ancient bookseller, grizzled with white hair he hadn't bothered to comb that morning, came to her aid.

"Miss Phyllis? You seem perplexed. Might I be of some assistance?"

"Hello Mr. Leto. How are you today?"

"Just fine, but I'm guessing you're in a bigger hurry than usual."

Phyllis grimaced. "Is it that obvious?"

He smiled. "Yes, so let me help you."

"Perhaps you could. I'm interested in reading these titles." She pointed at a row in the stacks. "But I'm having trouble choosing."

The short man pulled out a crisp handkerchief from his pocket. Watery eyes focused on the books as he delicately blotted the moisture. His glance at her was apologetic. "Allergies," he explained, as he always did. After tucking the hanky away, the man pulled a small book down from another shelf.

"Oh, but that's not where I'm looking, Mr. Leto," she began.

"Perhaps not, but I have a feeling this book will be much more enlightening for you."

She cocked a wary look at him. "How's that?"

He shrugged his shoulders before staring past at some unseen sight behind her. "It's not for me to say."

"But I'm interested in these other books." Phyllis pointed to her original shelf.

"Have I ever steered you wrong?" Before she could respond, he continued.

"Tell you what." The bookseller held up the book. "I'll give you this one for free."

Now she was really confused. "Why would you do that?"

"As I said...enlightening." With that, he turned to hobble slowly toward the cash register in the front of the store. He clutched a nearby table for support.

"Your leg seems better today."

He shrugged. "Sometimes it's good and sometimes I stay in one place."

"Was that from the first war?"

"Indeed, Miss Phyllis."

She glanced around the bookstore. "I still don't understand why you want to give me the book for nothing. You need money to keep the lights on." She smiled at him.

"I always manage. Now here." He held out the book. "Come back and talk to me after you've read it. I'll be interested in your critique. The writer is relatively new to American readers and his writing is first rate. I think you'll enjoy it."

For the first time, Phyllis glanced at the book in his hand. "*The Stranger* by Albert Camus."

"His name is pronounced Cam – oo, forgetting the s at the end."

"I stand corrected."

She accepted the book. At the cash register, he made some mysterious transaction before looking back to her.

"What is this fabulous-book-that-I-just-have-to-read about?" she said with a smile.

He nodded briefly. "It's the story of a man who must reconcile himself to the consequence of his actions."

"That's the theme, not the plot."

"It's woven together."

She laughed. "That's still not an answer, but apparently, it's all I'm going to get."

He nodded again. "Would you like a bag?"

"No. Thanks. I'll put it in my purse."

A tinkle of sound filled the air. The old bookseller looked toward the front door where a new customer was entering. With moisture collecting once again, he rubbed his eyes.

"Duty calls."

Phyllis glanced at her watch. "Mine too."

"Enjoy that book," he called out to her. She waved her response before leaving the old bookstore.

Outside on the sidewalk, Phyllis wondered for a brief moment what the heck that had been about until she remembered the time. If she weren't speedy, she'd be late for work. She tucked the book in her purse and thought no more about it.

"YOU'RE LATE."

Phyllis glanced at the clock on the wall. "By a whole two minutes, Mr. Martin."

"Two minutes late is still late." A stubby finger pointed in her direction.

He was really the most pathetic man. The scowl on his rodent-shaped face made deep lines in his forehead. His eyebrows pointed toward the recessed lines giving him a most unattractive look. His pouty expression might have been comical on anyone else. On him, comedy didn't resonate. He seemed built for unpleasantness; he sure reveled in it.

"Well, then I'll stay two minutes after work to make up the time."

That didn't impress him. "I don't know why, with all the people I have in my department, that I spend most of my time fretting about you."

Her eyes widened dramatically. "You fret about me? Why?"

"Maybe fret isn't the best word."

"What would be a better one?"

She stood her ground. By doing so, they were attracting a fair amount of attention. George Martin was a man who liked to throw his weight around. However, glancing at the stares from men and women working nearby, he was ready to change gears. This kind of attention wasn't going to do him any good. The personnel department had already received two complaints from other employees about his temper and his inability to control it.

He ran a fluttery hand along his bald head, smoothing a few lines in his forehead.

"This conversation is at a close, Mrs. Schneider. Perhaps you can get back to work on time and we'll have no further need for discussion of this kind."

"I'll do my best, Mr. Martin."

He nodded, grabbed a sheaf of papers from a desk and stalked back to his office. The door closed heavily behind him.

Immediately two of Phyllis' colleagues gathered around her.

"He's so terrible, Phyllis. What is his problem?" asked Barbara from two desks down.

"Yes," agreed Linda, a typist in the pool. "You seem to be singled out for his daily barrages."

Phyllis shook her head. "I don't get it either. I'm rarely late." She glanced toward the direction of Martin's office. "He doesn't seem to like me very much."

"He's just jealous," huffed Barbara.

"Of what?"

"Oh, Phyllis. Poo. You were an analyst at the American Embassy in London during the war and Oslo afterward. You have *credentials!*"

Linda nodded in agreement. "And Martin has never been posted anywhere but here in Washington. He can't stand that you have more experience than he does."

"And," continued Barbara, "he knows you compare him to your former bosses."

"No, I don't."

"Phyllis." Barbara and Linda gave her pitying looks. "How could you not?"

"Your boss in London was Major Richard Simpson," began Linda. "Why, everyone knows his record in Africa and London."

"Dickie was a good boss," agreed Phyllis.

"And don't forget Colonel Ronald Lawrence!" The women beamed at her. "You helped clear his name in that case of espionage and caught those ruffians with their war profiteering scheme."

"Well," Phyllis smiled. "Ronnie was a dear man who got caught up in circumstances beyond his control."

"They're both highly decorated military men who trusted you. You were able to do great things with your positions."

She blushed. "Let's not get crazy with praise here."

Linda angled her head. "We're just telling it as we've heard it. Do you deny any of what we've said?"

"No, but—"

"Then your actions stand." Linda and Barbara

crossed their arms across their chests and jutted out chins in defiance.

"I need to get to work."

Phyllis ducked around them, heading for her desk.

"See you later, Phyllis."

After the women had settled into their work, Phyllis thought about what they had said. She *did* have good experience behind her with solid officers who appreciated her work. What *was* Martin's problem?

She wanted to talk to Joe about what Barbara and Linda had said, but he would be gone to his therapist this afternoon when she got off work. Joe still suffered from battle fatigue due to his involvement with MI5 in London and a mission that had ended badly. Phyllis briefly considered calling Lorraine, her best friend, for a meet-up when her intercom buzzed.

"Mrs. Schneider? Would you come to the conference room please? Your presence has been requested."

Martin was summoning her to the conference room? Who had requested her attendance? Her position was that of a lowly secretary. Who in the world wanted her in a meeting?

Startled, Phyllis picked up her dictation pad and strode toward the conference room. This was a surprising turn of events. Her job didn't include going into top-secret meetings, which was what the conference room was used for. With no windows and a thick door that was usually locked, the whole office knew secrets were discussed there. Although uncertain, she held her head high, ignored the pointed looks from ladies in the pool, and knocked once on the heavy door.

When it opened, a familiar man with a big smile

thrust out his hand. She blinked in surprise and extended her hand in response.

"Get in here, Phyllis Bowden. You're late."

MAJOR RICHARD SIMPSON took her hand and pulled her into the room. She couldn't have been more surprised to see her former boss from the Embassy in London.

"Dickie!" She coughed. "Sorry, I mean, Major Simpson. What are you doing in Washington?"

"Ronnie says hello from Norway. He said to tell you he misses you."

It didn't escape her notice that her current boss, George Martin, sat at the table with three other men, two of them military officers. His face reflected resignation, along with a tinge of dismay. She knew immediately that he hadn't invited her.

"Come and sit down, Phyllis. I've missed you." His smile was contagious and she smiled back.

"You know that I'm not Phyllis Bowden anymore, don't you? Joe and I got married on board ship coming home."

He waved a hand. "Yes, yes. Anyway, whatever you're called now, we've decided to bring you in on today's meeting."

"Okay, thank you." *I think,* she thought but didn't say aloud. From the serious expressions in the room, she hadn't been invited to a tea party. Something big was happening, and she couldn't fathom why she'd been invited.

After she sat down, Dickie began introductions. Why was he taking charge instead of George Martin?

This wasn't Major Simpson's territory and the upper management in the CIA was very big on guarding their turf.

"You know George Martin."

"Of course." She nodded at Martin. "Sir."

He looked at her with little expression, his usual dull look.

Dickie waved toward the officers on her side of the table. "Captain Tom Metcalf and Major Pete Henderson, military intelligence." He nodded to the man next to George Martin. "Samuel Donohue, CIA."

He looked around the room. "Everyone introduced?" When he received nods, he took a chair at the head of the table. Another stunning move.

"You've been invited today, Phyllis, for a preliminary meeting."

"Did you want me to take notes, sir?"

He chuckled. "No." Dickie leaned forward on his arms. "What we want from you is your field expertise."

The surprise of seeing Major Simpson took back seat to the shock she received now. She hadn't been used as an agent since Oslo and then only under Col. Ronald Lawrence's direction, her boss then at the Embassy.

Phyllis tried hard to maintain her composure, although she felt the warmth spreading across her face. It wouldn't do to reveal her excitement. An assignment!

"I'm sure that news surprises you on a few fronts, Phyllis, so let me explain." Dickie glanced at Martin. "I've been transferred from London to a new position with Military Intelligence. We're coordinating with the Central Intelligence Agency for a special assignment."

"Yes, sir. How do I fit in?"

"Phyllis, what I'm about to tell you is top secret. You understand you're not to repeat anything said here to anyone outside of this room?"

"Of course, sir."

Dickie smoothed his tie before looking at each person around the table. Certain he had everyone's full attention, he began to speak in a calm, low voice. Phyllis moved forward in her chair to hear him properly.

"No note taking from anyone." With that command, Simpson took a deep breath. "There's a British physicist who is systematically giving secrets about the atomic bomb to the Russians. It hasn't been going on for very long, but we got a good tip and we're trying to trap him before he gives away too much information. So far, he has eluded us.

"We've received word that a company engineer who has worked with this scientist has documentation of his spying. The man has requested protection in exchange for his testimony."

He glanced around the room. "The decision has been made to nab the engineer before the Russian secret police are on to him. The plan in place will take a few months to set up, but we're confident he will be safe until we make our move. The main problem we see is that his wife is several months pregnant, maybe six. We don't want her in labor for this mission, so our window of opportunity is closing. Two months, gentlemen and lady." He smiled at Phyllis. "Two months to get this show on the road. It's essential this spy be caught."

Heads nodded in agreement. "Yes." "Certainly." "Absolutely." Other words showed support for the idea, making Phyllis aware that she was probably the last to know this information.

"Phyllis." Simpson looked at her. "We want you to capture the target."

"Excuse me?"

"We want you to pick up the engineer and his wife."

Phyllis took a deep breath. "Sir." She glanced around the table. "I've done jobs for Col. Lawrence, but nothing like this. Are you sure you want me and not a more experienced operative?"

George Martin looked like he was ready to agree with her.

"No, Phyllis. No one will ever suspect you. We're going to send you to work at the Oak Ridge Laboratory for the next two months while we flesh out the plan."

"You want me to go...to Tennessee, sir?"

"That's what we want."

"And this plan has been thoroughly discussed by everyone involved?"

"It has."

She sat back in her chair stunned. To her way of thinking, it was inconceivable that she should be chosen for such an important assignment. Martin hadn't given her much more than filing and a little dictation to do for the past year. He looked nearly as stunned as she. Perhaps he wasn't in on early discussions and the decisions made.

"Now, Phyllis, I know you'll have a million questions." Dickie nodded toward his audience. "These men have all the answers. I want you to report to another section of the agency for the upcoming week where you'll receive further instruction. Your job at the laboratory will be similar to your work here, so there will be no job stress." He smirked. "Well, not with that job anyway."

He waited until her shocked expression relaxed. "I know this may seem surprising, but it's been decided that you are the best agent for the assignment. That really shouldn't come as a surprise to you, after what you accomplished in London."

"Sir..."

"You should also know this mission is difficult to achieve under the best of circumstances. The engineer works for us, but we're fairly certain that the Russians are watching him for reasons we'll get into later. However, I think our plan, once it's in place, will be successful."

He sat back and smiled broadly. "Any questions?"

It was a good thing Phyllis was sitting down. Her legs, quivering like jelly, wouldn't be able to hold her up. "Lots, sir. When do we start?"

"Tomorrow morning you report to Level 5. You need to get a new badge before tomorrow. Your clearance has been upgraded as well. That's it for now, Miss Bowden, er, I mean, Mrs. Schneider." He stood and held out his hand.

The other men stood as well.

Phyllis rose and shook Dickie's hand. Glancing at George Martin, she nodded.

"Thank you, sir."

With that, Phyllis left the room trying not to float on fluffy clouds. An assignment as an agent! She'd trained and trained for field positions and had felt thwarted that she received so few. It was a chance to prove herself on her home turf. She was thrilled and excited. Also slightly terrified.

And she couldn't tell Joe.

PHYLLIS STAYED five minutes over quitting time, just to appease George Martin. Since he wasn't around when she left, her time had been wasted, but who knew? Maybe he had a spy camera pointed at the typing pool, hoping to catch some unwary rule-bender.

She and Lorraine, her best friend, rode the same streetcar after work, so they caught up on the latest gossip. Suzy from Operations upstairs just got engaged. Lorraine wasn't pleased about this happy news since she and Henry had been engaged for a while now.

"So why don't you and Henry get married?" asked Phyllis. "What's the hold-up?"

Lorraine rolled her eyes. "You know very well that we can't decide on the venue. I've suggested either the Willard or Jefferson Hotels because they're so beautiful and utterly perfect for our wedding."

"Wow! Pricey."

"That's what Henry says too. He wants to go down to the courthouse for the ceremony and have a party in one of the parks."

"Really?" Phyllis tried to stop her grin. "That's the extreme in the opposite direction."

"Tell me about it." Lorraine frowned, then grabbed onto the seat when the streetcar suddenly lurched. "We go round and round and end up in a big fight."

"Well, maybe if you—"

"Tell me," Lorraine interrupted, "why I wanted to marry this guy in the first place. Remember all the dates I had in London?"

"Yes, sweetie. You've been a southern belle of the ball."

"I liked being the belle of the ball."

"Sure, you want to get married then?" Phyllis looked over at Lorraine to check her expression.

Lorraine's pretty face brightened from a scowl to a beaming smile. "I guess I do. Henry is the best thing that's ever happened to me."

"And considering the territory you took in, that's saying a mouthful!"

Their quick laughter filled the small streetcar. Looks from other passengers were curious.

"All right, then. Get back to the drawing board and come up with something different," Phyllis suggested.

"Maybe you're right. You do get it right from time to time."

"Sure. I married Joe, didn't I?"

Lorraine poked her in the arm. "Some girls get all the luck. He had his eye on you the first time you met. In fact, he had his eye on you before you met. Remember? He asked me to introduce the two of you at a party."

"In exchange for taking a drunk Henry home," Phyllis reminded her with a smirk.

"Okay. Memory Lane is closed." Lorraine glanced out the window. "Here's my stop. See you tomorrow."

"Night."

Phyllis watched her friend depart the streetcar. She gave her head a half-hearted shake. Wartime romances had a bad reputation, but Lorraine and Henry really were a good match. She knew Lorraine had a wild streak, and Henry seemed able to roll with the punches to keep her in line, when she needed to be. They'd be able to work out any problems that came along. She felt sure about it.

Phyllis closed her eyes and thought about the meeting today in the conference room. Her new assignment had floated down from CIA heaven. She was thrilled and terrified, happy and spooked. She needed to talk to someone about it, but she knew she couldn't tell Joe. Even though he was in intelligence himself and had been for years, she knew he'd understand, when the assignment was over, why she held back from him.

But it wasn't settling smoothly in her gut.

Maybe tomorrow, after reporting for work at the new location, she would be able to get the answers she needed and talk everything over with someone who knew the score.

Staring out the window, she realized her stop was coming up. Her small house was in a relatively new neighborhood that was perfect for them. Phyllis smiled. Home. The perfect place to be when life needed soothing. Joe would be home soon. Thank goodness for that. The man knew her inside out and could extinguish most fires with a sexy smile or knowing look.

She stepped off the streetcar.

THE SMALL WOODEN chip wasn't in the doorframe.

She and Joe, both trained agents, used the chip to warn them in advance of uninvited guests. And like the trained agent she was, Phyllis glanced around before pulling the derringer from her purse. Pushing open the front door, her senses alert for the slightest movement, she briefly appreciated the rays of sun bursting through the window above the door. It gave her the light she needed before venturing a foot farther.

Once inside, she closed the door quietly, noting the hallway with a quick look: the floral wallpaper, the hall tree waiting by the door for her coat. The tiled floor showed slight footprints in the dust that she hadn't swept away. Fragments of the footprints led to the living room where she ventured slowly, gun in hand.

Everything looked the same as she had left it this morning. The worn striped carpet over the hardwood floor hadn't been disturbed, nor had the old upright piano and its swivel stool. The velour couch that Joe's mother had given them had a slight indentation on the right side, catching Phyllis' attention and worry.

A small movement from the kitchen had Phyllis' gun aimed in that direction instantly.

A figure in dark clothing held up his hands.

"Don't shoot me, Phyllis."

She recognized his voice. "Col. Lawrence!"

"In the flesh."

For a moment she was speechless. She watched as her former boss took a step closer, but only a step.

"I was surprised by Major Simpson this morning and now you! I thought you were in Oslo!"

"That is what we wanted you and everyone else to think."

"But sir..."

"May I put my hands down?"

"Of course." Phyllis lowered her gun, tucked it safely into her purse. "But why would you want me to think that you're in Oslo when you're not?"

"Come in the kitchen, Phyllis. I bet this is where you and Joe have your important discussions."

She smiled. "It is and I'm not going to ask how you knew that."

Col. Ronald Lawrence smiled back at her. "Just as well."

"You're not in uniform."

"No. The job was too important to announce my presence to the community."

"What job, sir?"

He waved a hand toward the kitchen table.

"See? I found Joe's whiskey and already poured us each a glass."

She walked to the table, pulled out a chair across from Col. Lawrence.

"So, we're celebrating?"

"You've been handed an important assignment, Phyllis."

"You know about that?"

He indicated she should sit.

"It's of the utmost importance that this spy be caught. He's done enough damage to the project already. We fear the Soviets have more information than they are entitled to."

"Why would a British physicist willingly give over atomic secrets to the Russians? What would be his motive?" She picked up the glass Ronnie had poured for her.

"Many scientists on both sides of the ocean have had Communist leanings for years. Some decry foul against those men who have decided to use their scientific knowledge for weaponry. These scientists prefer everyone would stick to science for its own sake, not for war."

"Even when Hitler was in the picture, also trying to build a bomb?"

"Even then and now we have Stalin in the picture. The scientist being sought is a good friend of well-known pacifists, although he was never one himself. He feels his friends have good intentions about not wanting to use their research for war purposes, but they are delusional. The man thinks that peace will be secured only if the major countries involved on the world scene have the atomic bomb. And that's the US and the Soviet Union. Only then can peace be guaranteed."

"Seems naïve."

"Perhaps so, but that is his thinking according to his friends and family." He cocked his head at her. "He may also be under the influence of a special friend, someone with a large reputation within the community."

Phyllis smiled. "I've heard some about that. Have many resources gone into this project?"

"The scientist has been followed for the past year and much is known about his activities."

"Why hasn't he been caught before now?"

Ronnie raised his glass and grinned. Phyllis noted his clear, forthright eyes had deep recesses underneath. Something was keeping him up nights.

She raised her glass to his.

"Are we working together again, sir?"

"No, Phyllis. I'm just here to wish you good luck. Major Simpson sneaked me in under the proverbial radar, so I could give you a proper send-off on your first real assignment here in the States."

"I appreciate it, Colonel."

He clinked his glass to hers. "Here's to a job well-done."

"Thank you, sir."

Ronnie drained his glass in one gulp as Phyllis sipped hers.

"Go on, Phyllis Bowden. Swallow that sucker."

She laughed and drained it. The fiery liquid burned its way down her throat causing her to cough and Lawrence to smile. It was good to see him again.

"To answer that last question, let me say this. He hasn't been caught because we've lacked the evidence needed to prove his treasonous acts."

"And the engineer has the evidence?"

"He does."

She toyed with the glass, tilting it to one side. "If I may be allowed to ask, what then is your involvement in this assignment?"

"Major Simpson asked for my advice before assigning this to you, Phyllis." With the look on her face, he hastily continued. "Not that he didn't feel you could handle the work, but your Washington boss wasn't easily convinced."

"I know George Martin doesn't like me very much, Colonel."

"You came with excellent recommendations from both myself and Major Simpson."

"Apparently, he wasn't impressed."

Ronnie laughed, poured another glass of whiskey. He held the bottle over her glass. "Another for you?"

"No, thanks. Joe will come home wondering why I was drinking in the afternoon. I don't like to lie."

"I don't blame you. It's tough, sometimes in our job, trying to explain things to loved ones. Joe's an agent himself and should understand when things seem inexplicable."

"He does, most of the time."

"Most of the time?" His eyebrows arched in question.

"He still suffers from battle fatigue, sir. That Romanian assignment nearly did him in. He has the occasional episode and not always at convenient times."

Ronnie nodded solemnly. "Yes, I understand. It took many brave men and women to defeat the enemy. We didn't all come back in one piece. Is he receiving the treatment he needs?"

"Yes."

"Well, good." He drank down his whiskey and stood up. "I need to leave before he gets home. My presence would be too hard to explain."

Phyllis grinned. "I'll say."

"Walk me to the door."

"The front door, sir?"

"It's the way I came in. Your neighbors might suspect you're having an affair if I sneak out the back."

She ducked her head to hide the blush she knew was creeping across her face.

Ronnie stopped to pull something from an inside coat pocket. "I brought this for you, Miss Bowden."

"Mrs. Schneider."

"You'll always be Miss Bowden to me, Phyllis."

He opened his hand. "Take this."

She looked at the object in his hand. "But I have a compact already."

"Not like this one. Take it."

When she had it in her hand, Ronnie continued. "Open it and move it around to see what you see."

Phyllis moved the mirror to different angles until a message appeared. Startled, she asked, "What's this?"

"Directions to the safe house where you'll be taking the target. Keep it on you always."

"I thought I would be receiving this and other instructions next week."

"You will, but the safe house was mine to give you. I want you to come back safe and sound, so Major Simpson gave me the honor."

She smiled at him. He was really the best of men. "Thank you, sir. It was an honor to work for you."

"*With* me, Phyllis. You worked *with* me."

With that, Col. Ronald Lawrence, Military Attaché in the American Embassy in Oslo, Norway, pulled out a cap and smoothed it on his head. "How do I look?"

"Like a man about to hop in his sports car."

"More's the better for the deceit." He paused to take her in once more. "Godspeed, Mrs. Schneider."

"And to you, sir."

He slipped out the door, probably as quietly as he had slipped in. Leaning with her back against it, Phyllis breathed deeply and wondered, not for the first time, just how dangerous her upcoming assignment would be. She shook her head of unwanted thoughts. This was her job. This is what she was trained to do.

Glancing at the grandfather clock in the hallway, she knew she had another job to do right now: dinner. Joe would be home shortly and she had to maintain a normal composure, through her excitement and anxiety. If not, Joe would know her secret.

And that just wouldn't do.

. . .

SHE NOTICED it when he walked in the door. Joe didn't call out to her, as he usually did. His footsteps down the hall were all she heard of him.

He was so habitual that any slight change in routine signaled that something was off. Glancing out the kitchen at him, she watched Joe stop before going into the bedroom to pull a limp hanky from his pants pocket. She could see the perspiration dripping down his face from a few feet away. He wouldn't want her to see him like this, so she popped back into the kitchen. She washed the two glasses used by Col. Lawrence and herself, and left the whiskey bottle on the kitchen table, placing a new glass beside it. Joe might not want her to know what had happened, but he would soon realize she'd learn anyway. There were no secrets between them.

Until today.

She got out a pan, making more noise than she usually would, and placed it on the stove. Gathering ingredients for a pot roast, she hastily set about slicing potatoes, carrots and onions. She clunked the pan with a spoon unnecessarily, filling the kitchen with more culinary noises. Just as she was sprinkling the beef with salt and pepper, Joe stepped into the kitchen.

"Oh! Joe! You're home!" She tried to keep her expression light, but he wasn't fooled.

"Which you knew, honey. You saw me in the hallway."

"What? Have you eyes in the back of your head?"

"No, but there's a mirror right where I was standing. I saw you clear as day."

"Joe, I—"

He took out his handkerchief again to mop his sweaty face. "It's okay."

"No, it isn't." She moved closer to take the hanky from him. Gently blotting his face, his arms went around her to pull her close.

"It's okay because I'm here with you."

"Did you have an episode today at work?"

He nodded. "Someone dropped a glass at a meeting, which triggered it. The glass splintering into a thousand pieces nearly had me splintered. I had to go to the men's room to get myself under control."

"What did you do?"

"I stuck my head, as far as I could," he added when she smiled, "under a faucet in the sink. It was ridiculous, but brought me back around."

Phyllis tucked the hanky back in Joe's pocket. Her eyes skimmed his handsome face. Clear blue eyes with a hint of sadness, his downturned lips and dark hair already tinged with gray told the story. Joe Schneider had suffered much in the war as a British agent. After that grueling incident in Bucharest, he'd thrown in the towel and admitted he couldn't do the job any longer. She knew when they'd married that he might always suffer from the battle fatigue symptoms he'd acquired after that last assignment. But being young, she figured they could work anything out together.

Now she wasn't so sure.

Maybe their love wasn't the panacea Joe needed. He was going to a therapist on a regular basis, but, after more than a year of therapy, Joe's episodes didn't seem to be lessening. He needed something else; something they hadn't thought of.

Joe drew her in closer. When their lips met, all

thoughts went out of her head. As their kiss deepened with love and gratitude, her eyes moistened at the thought of possibly losing him. She grabbed him tightly and held on for dear life.

No. It was unthinkable.

She looked away when their lips moved apart, so she could hastily wipe her eyes.

"Phyllis? Are you crying?"

"No! Of course not. I just cut up an onion for the pot roast."

Although his slight frown signaled, he didn't believe her. Joe let it go.

"What time will dinner be ready?"

"We have an hour."

"Good. I'm going to change clothes. Let's have coffee out on the deck."

"It's getting cold outside, Joe."

"The coffee will warm us."

She opened her mouth to complain, but he smiled and left the room. When she heard water running in the bathroom, Phyllis put the roast in the oven and set the controls. She glanced at the whiskey on the table. Maybe she'd put a tumbler in their coffee.

Tidying up, she remembered sitting in her mother's kitchen talking about her day at school. Hurtful slights from other children had wounded a young Phyllis, but they seemed trivial compared to her life today. Being snubbed by Trudy What's-her-name in the fourth grade cut deeply when she was nine years old. But was that any different than being patronized by George Martin now that she was approaching thirty?

Both cuts wounded her psyche and made her doubt

her value as a person. Hadn't she learned anything in twenty-some years of living?

She could see a lot of her mother in herself. Phyllis' father was ill for a major part of his adult life with one problem after another. Now cancer was slowly draining the life from him. But she'd watched how her father's illnesses drained the life out of her mother over time. Constance Bowden had died of a heart attack at only fifty years old. Sliding a wet cloth along the kitchen countertop, Phyllis wondered how her mother was able to deal with illness day in, day out.

And where was she now when she needed her mother's advice so badly about Joe? Was she turning into her mother? Was her life with Joe becoming a repeat of her mother's life?

Phyllis shook her head. She threw the wet cloth in the sink a little harder than she meant to. Constance had done her duty by her husband, yet much of life had passed her by because of it. She was most proud of her two daughters. Phyllis had gone to college and had taken a job at the Pentagon just before her mother died. Her sister had married and given birth to two children, which had thrilled their mother.

Phyllis' chin jutted out. She was not becoming her sainted mother. She and Joe would put the battle fatigue behind them and live their lives the best way they knew.

An errant thought crossed her mind: children.

She and Joe had never discussed having children. Maybe it was time to start. The smile she caught reflecting off the shiny coffee pot turned to a frown. Here she was an agent with the Central Intelligence Agency about to go on a dangerous assignment and she was thinking about having a child? Was she nuts? She was certainly losing her focus.

Phyllis got a pot of coffee brewing just in time to hear Joe's call.

"Honey? Ready with the coffee?"

"Just about, Joe. I'll meet you out back."

She snagged a sweater from the hall tree, poured two cups and walked down the hallway to meet him.

"So how was your day?" asked Joe when she passed him a cup.

She was saved momentarily from answering when he sipped his coffee and his eyes widened comically. "Sweetie, did you put whiskey in this?"

Phyllis didn't have a ready answer for either of Joe's questions.

ONCE THEY WERE SETTLED in the swing on their back porch, Joe coughed and took a gulp of his coffee. His infectious grin was immediate.

"You should buy this brand of coffee always at the store, honey. It's a big improvement on that stuff you usually get."

His teasing relaxed her.

"It's chilly out tonight. I thought a little whiskey would warm you up faster."

He licked his lips. "I'm plenty warm now. Thanks."

That was one answer to his questions. What could she say about the other?

"So how was your day, dear?"

"No, you first. I already mentioned the meeting when I had a small episode."

She stalled. "Surely that wasn't the only thing that happened today."

"Phyllis, you can't hide from me. I'll tell you all about my lackluster day, as soon as you come clean about yours. Come on. Tell me."

Wracking her brain for a suitable distraction, she finally hit on it.

"I was two minutes late coming back from lunch today and George Martin made a scene about it."

Joe set down his cup. "What did he say?"

"That he was bothered by my lateness and he fretted over me more than his other employees."

"He said that? Out loud with others listening?"

"He did."

"What an ass."

"I thought so too. I told him I'd stay two minutes over quitting time, which I did, but he was gone and wouldn't know if I left a half hour early."

He thought about that, took another sip of his cooling coffee.

"I suppose Linda and Barbara had something to say."

"Sure. They pointed out, with everyone listening, that I had great credentials from my past postings." She took a sip. "It was kind of embarrassing how they went on and on."

Joe laughed. "Oh, you love it and you know it."

That earned him a smile. Phyllis wondered how to bring up the Tennessee assignment. She'd need a cover story for the reason she'd be going there.

"So how was your day?"

He shot her a side look. She couldn't read his expression.

Joe sighed. "I thought working as a temporary consultant with the agency until my US citizenship came through would be a piece of cake."

"Isn't it?"

"My boss thinks going from being an MI5 agent to the CIA should be fairly easy and I would want to continue doing what I've done in the past. He was making noises today about sending me back in the field, once I get the all-clear."

"And you don't want that?"

He reached out to touch her face. "I'm liking my desk job a whole bunch, honey. It's dangerous out in the field."

"You don't trust yourself to do more than you're doing?"

"No. Honestly, I don't."

She swallowed. "Okay, that's your answer then. Tell your boss no."

"Could you say no to your boss?"

"George Martin? Oh, yes."

Joe chuckled at her tough stance.

"Yes, I believe you could. You're much tougher than me, Phyllis Schneider."

"I'm a pussy cat and you know it." She leaned over to touch his lips with hers.

"You're certainly a pretty one. I know that." He kissed her back, taking time to settle their lips with familiarity.

A wind picked up, blowing her hair around her face. Phyllis shivered.

"Let's go back in. It's getting colder."

Long after dinner, when they'd gone to bed, Phyllis was startled out of a deep sleep by a shrill cry.

Shaking off her sleepiness, she raised up to pull Joe to her.

"Honey! Wake up! You're having a nightmare."

She shook his shoulders gently, watching his troubled face. Whatever demons were disturbing his sleep had him well and truly in their grasp. She shook him until his eyes opened.

"Phyllis?"

"Yes, Joe. Are you awake now?"

She waited until his unfocused eyes stared straight at her with recognition. When she knew he was seeing her and not the apparition in his head, she smiled and kissed him.

"Joe? Honey? You all right?"

Joe breathed deeply, glanced around the room. She knew he was settling back into his surroundings.

"You okay? Would you like some water?"

"Yes, please."

She kept a glass on the nightstand for nights like these. Reaching over, she brought the glass to him. He drank deeply.

After handing the glass back, Joe sank back into the bed with a shivering sigh she felt in her bones.

"All right now?"

"I just told Dr. Thompson this afternoon that the episodes were lessening." He shook his head, looked over at her. "But I was right back in that room tonight, Phyllis, being grilled by the Soviet spy and shot by the Romanian."

It had taken Joe the better part of a year to finally tell Phyllis the whole story of his captivity. Extended amnesia, after his release, let Joe avoid any explanations for a while. Once therapy began and his memory

returned, his doctors gently suggested that he tell
Phyllis as much as he was able. She had reacted the way
she thought she would: she cried. Buckets. In his presence and when he was gone. His inhumane treatment
caused her much grief, so much that she tried to wipe
his words from her mind. It was a never-ending battle to
clean that slate.

Especially during times of incredible stress like
now. Joe was suffering and there was little she could do
to help him. But her presence seemed to have a soothing
effect, and for that, she was grateful. So, she would be
here for him.

Wait a minute. How would she be here for him if
she were in Tennessee?

TWO

COMPLICATIONS

Her schedule for her first week of training was packed. She'd reported to level five of the main building of the CIA where security procedures were doubled and tripled. Her new badge apparently didn't impress the guard on the fifth level, even though her picture was on it, along with her higher security clearance. He took his time checking her purse and briefcase as if she were the spy being discussed in all her top-level meetings.

The first meeting of the first day was an eye-opener. Major Dick Simpson paced the length of the conference table back and forth, barely sparing the meeting's participants a glance. His green wool jacket was laid on the arm of a chair. His dark tie was askew, as though he'd been tugging at it in frustration. She presumed a laundress had labored to iron his shirt, since it looked starched and crisp. However, perspiration stains circling the armpits showed Dickie's obvious anxiety.

"Sir? Do you need a glass of water?" Phyllis reached for the pitcher in front of her. Dickie stopped her.

"No, Phyllis, but thanks. I have a lot on my mind."

"Of course." She sat back, waiting for him to start the meeting.

Finally, Major Simpson sat stiffly in a chair near the end of the table, away from the three other people, including Phyllis.

She wondered what was bothering him.

"Tom?"

"Sir?"

"Would you begin your briefing?"

"Sure." Col. Metcalf, his Army uniform more polished than Simpson's today, stood to hand out a small stack of papers.

"This is Graham Gresham."

Phyllis took one of the sheets to observe the picture of a slim, dark-haired man wearing round, wire spectacles and an ill-fitting suit. He was standing by a table filled with other men, scientists probably, and a chalkboard in the background. The man looked as if he were seriously contemplating what another man was saying. A pipe stem poked out of his jacket pocket. His demeanor was so ordinary and professorial that she would never have figured him to be a spy giving secrets about the atomic bomb to the Russians.

She laid the picture on the table and looked up at Col. Metcalf.

"Gresham holds a doctorate in physics from the University of Oxford. He's held posts as lecturer at several universities before being asked to participate in the building of the atomic bomb. He worked on the Manhattan Project for a while and then was transferred as a researcher to Oak Ridge."

"Sir?" asked Phyllis. "Oak Ridge?"

"Yes," replied Metcalf. "Oak Ridge National Laboratory is in Oak Ridge, Tennessee, in the eastern part of the state, and is a division of the Department of Energy. After the Manhattan Project researchers developed the atomic bomb, one of the main goals for the lab in Oak Ridge was to channel the power of the atom for peaceful purposes."

His expression remained neutral, but his lips quirked.

"After the uranium bomb, the plutonium bomb came along, which you all know. Researchers at Oak Ridge are leaders in developing nuclear technology. There are those at the facility who see peaceful purposes for this technology, but so far it's only been used for weaponry." He glanced around the room. "Dr. Gresham, the spy we're seeking, definitely saw the war potential and has been feeding secrets to the Soviets for longer than we know."

"How has this information come to us, Col. Metcalf?" A man in a gray-striped suit looked out of place with a table filled with Army officers. Since introductions had been sketchy, she guessed he was CIA.

"Dr. Leahy, this information has come from an engineer who just happens to be the spy's brother."

"His brother?" exclaimed Leahy.

"Yes."

"Most extraordinary."

"That's what we thought. Anyway, the engineer is the man we are hoping to extract and debrief."

Phyllis didn't look around, but she felt brief gazes from the others in the room. That was her job. It's why she was here. Her lips felt uncommonly dry.

Col. Metcalf continued his briefing about Dr. Gresham. Questions were asked from others at the table, but Phyllis just listened. She knew she'd need as much information as possible to help catch such a wily operative. Gazing at Gresham's photo, she snapped to attention with a comment made by Leahy.

"Mole, Tom? Dr. Gresham is a mole?"

"We believe so," replied Metcalf. He reached for other papers to distribute. "Here's an in-depth biography of Gresham and his immediate family. He was born into English society to well-to-do parents. His father demanded much of his son when his scientific abilities were recognized. At university, Gresham majored in electrical engineering and eventually physics for an advanced degree. His career was skyrocketing when he was tapped to assist with Manhattan Project research at Oak Ridge. His family sent a brother over with him and that's who contacted the head of Oak Ridge security about a possible leak."

"His brother? Really?" asked Phyllis.

"Yes, he's an engineer also assigned at Oak Ridge. He apparently has been used by the family to help Dr. Gresham."

"Help him with what?"

Metcalf cocked his head at Phyllis.

"The man is a magnet for trouble."

"What kind of trouble?"

"Drinking, carousing, womanizing."

Phyllis almost choked. "He doesn't sound like your typical atomic scientist."

"No indeed. But that's the dossier on him."

"When did he begin spying for the Russians?"

"Not long after he got a fellow scientist's daughter pregnant."

Phyllis blinked. No one around the table moved.

"And then what happened?" she asked.

"She has been a troublemaker herself and got tangled up with the Russians. It's a long story and her father has been implicated as well. She coerced Gresham into doing a little spying to spring him from blackmail. Gresham caved and then he couldn't get out."

"The brother told all of this?"

"Yes."

Phyllis sat back stunned. It flew in the face of all she knew about loyalty to country and family.

"That's good for now, Tom. Thank you."

Metcalf took a seat.

"Anyone have any further questions?"

More questions and answers were batted around the table for a good long while. When the questions dried up, Simpson called the meeting to a halt.

"Enough for now. How about we break for lunch and be back here at two o'clock?"

"Two, sir?" Phyllis glanced at her watch.

"That should be time enough to find out what Lorraine is doing." Dickie smirked at her faint blush.

"Thank you, sir." Phyllis gathered her materials in a briefcase. She immediately checked it into a locked storage room before taking the elevator down to the first floor. She headed for the ladies' restroom by the cafeteria where she and Lorraine had arranged to meet to freshen up before going to lunch.

"YOU DON'T LOOK SO GOOD."

"Thanks a bunch. Thought you were going to cheer me up."

"Why do you need cheering up, Phyllis?" Lorraine looked at her friend's reflection in the bathroom mirror. "Is George Martin yammering at you again?"

Phyllis swallowed hard. Something in her throat just wouldn't go down. She blotted her face with a wet paper towel. The meetings about her assignment weren't scaring her. In fact, it was the opposite. Phyllis felt energized with each new piece of information. But the sudden headache and fluttering in her stomach told a different story.

"Or is Joe having more episodes?" Lorraine clamped a hand on Phyllis' arm. "You're cold." She reached up to lay a hand on Phyllis' forehead. "But your head feels warm. You must be catching a cold."

"Maybe I am. Maybe I just need to—" Before she could finish, Phyllis turned abruptly to push into a bathroom stall. With the door closed behind her, sounds of retching filled the bathroom.

"Jeez, Phyllis. You *are* sick!" Lorraine pushed the door open to see her friend huddled over a toilet. "I'll get you a towel."

It was several minutes before Phyllis could respond in any way to Lorraine's inquiries. Finally, she was able to drag herself back to a sink to use the damp towel Lorraine pressed into her hand.

"Thanks."

"You look terrible, hon." Lorraine peered at her. "You aren't pregnant, are you?"

"No." Phyllis splashed water on her face. She and Joe had been very careful with their lovemaking, but it wasn't information she was willing to share with her friend.

"You sure? When was your last period?"

"Lorraine!"

"Oh, poo. We've been friends forever. You can tell me."

Phyllis sighed. She could trust Lorraine with most things.

"Well, it was..." She trailed off when she couldn't remember when she'd had her last period. "It was three weeks ago, or was it four?"

"You really don't remember? Honey." Lorraine turned Phyllis to look at her. "Then there's a chance."

"No, absolutely not. Joe and I..." She didn't finish the sentence on purpose.

"You know we've discussed ways to keep from getting pregnant."

"Um, yes."

Lorraine continued babbling. "But you know they don't always work. Mabel in Accounting got pregnant with the rhythm method."

Phyllis smiled. "You know we aren't Catholic, Lorraine."

"Oh, that's right. I've always used a diaphragm, but Cindy in Operations said she found a hole in hers."

Her comment caused Phyllis' face to pale even more. Lorraine caught her reaction.

"Honey. Is that what you're using?"

"I don't want to talk about it." Although she did *think* about it. It was all she *could* think about. She and Joe had used condoms recently since her doctor suggested she replace the diaphragm she'd been using. Maybe there had been a hole in hers like Cindy's in Accounting.

Lorraine studied Phyllis' reflection as her friend put on lipstick and combed her hair.

"You really should see a doctor, Phyl. It could be serious. One doesn't just upchuck for no reason."

The longer Phyllis ran a comb through her hair, the sharper Lorraine's expression became. "You *are* pregnant, Phyllis. I've got a feeling about this."

"You're always getting weird feelings."

"I'm on the money with this one. I'd bet my marriage to Henry."

Phyllis looked her in the eye. "Are you that sure?"

"Yes."

It took less than a minute for Phyllis' eyes to fill with tears. "I can't be pregnant," she whined.

"Why not?"

"It's just...it's not a...good time."

A slow smile spread across Lorraine's face. "Is there ever a good time? Sometimes these things just happen."

Phyllis fished a tissue from her purse. "Pregnancy doesn't just happen."

"Well, that's true enough." She looked at her friend sharply. "Are you worried about Joe?"

"I'm usually worried about Joe."

"I thought the battle fatigue was lessening."

"It comes and goes."

"He will be thrilled to pieces, Phyl. Just go to a doctor. Make sure and then tell Joe the good news."

Phyllis swallowed. "You really think I could be pregnant?"

"I think there's a strong possibility."

"Oh, boy."

Lorraine grinned. "Be happy when you say that! You're having a baby!"

Phyllis' stomach lurched again at the news and had

her dashing back into a bathroom stall. Lorraine smiled happily.

"And I get to be the crazy aunt!"

Phyllis flushed the toilet and thought she saw her career being flushed too.

WITH PREGNANCY ON HER MIND, the last thing Phyllis needed was a call from her sister. Before heading back into a meeting, she picked up the phone with one hand on her stomach.

"Phyllis?"

"Hi Connie."

"I haven't heard from you in ages. Why do I always have to be the one who keeps in touch?"

Phyllis sighed, then glanced at her watch. "I have approximately seven minutes before I have to go to a meeting. What's up?"

"I need to talk to you about Dad."

"We spoke last week."

"...He's worse, sis. When did you see him last?"

"Joe and I went by two weeks ago, but I've called him several times since then."

"Did he answer the phone?"

"The phone rang and rang the last time before he picked up."

"He fell yesterday and is back in the hospital."

Phyllis covered her mouth with her hand. "Oh no! Is he all right?"

"No. Look. We need to talk. When do you have some time?"

Crap. When *did* she have some time? Between prepping for her new assignment, Joe's therapy sessions and now a new doctor appointment of her own, Phyllis couldn't think of any minutes in the next day or two that weren't already booked.

"Tomorrow? What have you got going on tomorrow?"

"Connie, I can't think of my schedule right this minute. I'm rattled about Dad. Could I call you later?"

"Absolutely. Tonight, when you get home?"

"Yes."

"Good. I'll talk to you then."

Phyllis hung up with more fluttering in her stomach. She was stuck between going to her meeting or dashing to the nearest restroom. She took a few deep breaths, calmed her stomach and walked to the elevator.

Life could wait. She had a job to do.

A FEW DAYS LATER, the streetcar lurched suddenly, throwing Phyllis onto the dirty floor. Lorraine helped her up, having kept her seat by grabbing the man next to her, to his obvious disapproval. She slapped on a brave smile as she pulled Phyllis back to her seat.

"Thanks, mister."

"You nearly tore my jacket, miss." His sneer only succeeded in making Lorraine laugh.

"Nearly only counts in horseshoes, pal."

Phyllis smoothed her overcoat and reached up to feel for her new earrings. Joe had given them to her for their anniversary and she hoped she hadn't lost them. They were still in place.

"Lorraine." Her sharp tone steered Lorraine's attention away from the snarling man next to her.

"What?"

"Can't you ever..." But her sentence was left unfinished. Glancing past Lorraine, Phyllis pointed. "My book fell out."

"What are you looking at? That book?"

"Yeah."

"Looks boring. Did you get it recently?"

"...Um. Last week, I think. I forgot I had it."

Lorraine pushed back the pale hair from her face when she bent over to pick up the book. "Strange title. What's it about?"

"I'm not sure."

"You picked it out, didn't you?"

"Not exactly."

"Phyllis, you're not making any sense." Lorraine's eyes dropped to the floor. "What's that?" A piece of yellow paper had slipped out of the book. Lorraine picked it up delicately with two fingers.

Phyllis looked over her shoulder. "That's my question."

"Look." They stared at the paper. "It's got your name on it."

"What?"

By this time, even the displeased man next to Lorraine was watching their every move. Phyllis plucked the note from Lorraine to stuff it in her coat pocket.

"I'll read it later."

"Don't you want to know what it says?"

The man next to Lorraine nodded.

"Because I sure do."

Phyllis glanced down at the paper in her hand. A plain, single-folded sheet of paper, not much bigger than a matchbook, bore her name. *Phyllis Bowden.* That was odd. She had married Joe last year and had changed her name to Schneider. The print was in tiny block print, like an architect's handwriting. Lorraine nudged her impatiently.

"Go on. Open it."

With hesitation, Phyllis opened the note.

Don't do it.

She read the message again before turning the paper over to see if anything was written on the other side. Nothing.

"Don't do it?" read Lorraine. "Don't do what?"

The man next to Lorraine was reading over her shoulder like Lorraine was reading over Phyllis'. Both sets of wide eyes fixed on Phyllis for her answer.

"I haven't the foggiest."

Lorraine shot a "Back off" look at the nosy man, who settled in his seat, pulling up his newspaper in front of his face.

She lowered her voice and whispered to Phyllis. "Something about work?"

Phyllis breathed shakily. It could very well be about work, but she couldn't tell that to Lorraine.

"Hardly. George won't give me anything much to do. I've been filing again this week."

"Huh. Probably somebody in your office having some fun."

"That's not very likely." Then she remembered where she got the book—from the old bookseller.

Lorraine waved a hand. "It's somebody playing a joke, that's all."

"Seems like an odd joke."

Lorraine rolled her eyes. "Well, I don't know, but listen. I've got bigger fish to fry than some silly note."

Her eyes took on a faraway look. "I was thinking of changing my hairstyle for the wedding. What do you think? I'm tired of the same old victory rolls and I wanted to have Marcy give me a pageboy. I was at the beauty parlor last week and I saw a style that was positively dreamy."

Lorraine's voice faded to a low background hum. Phyllis' mind wandered as she watched the tall federal buildings go by outside the window across from her seat. Classic architecture made of granite and steel with Roman columns holding a V-shaped roof. Newer buildings were more modern with curved designs, but white or beige still remained the popular color. She noted one building looked tiringly like the other, but eventually, neighborhoods with trees and children playing would appear.

And she'd be home.

Her mind zoomed back to the present.

Huh.

Don't do it. That's what the note said. What the devil could that mean? Don't do what?

A task at work?

Don't read this book?

Don't make pot roast for dinner anymore?

It could possibly mean a million things, but the longer she sat in the bumpy streetcar, listening to Lorraine go on and on about her hair, the more she decided the message was directed at her latest assignment. Her name was on it, her maiden name at that, meaning the warning was from someone who had known her for at least a year.

A shiver worked its way down her spine as she glanced around the crowded streetcar.

"Phyllis? Are you listening to me?"

"Ah, sure. Continue with what you were saying."

"But it's needs to be a soft pageboy. Why, last week in the cafeteria, I saw..."

Phyllis' mind wandered again. Where had the book come from? Oh, yes. She'd gotten it in that old bookstore down the street from the drugstore. The old bookseller had insisted that she take it. He had even given it to her for free. Was the note from him?

That was a possibility.

And if it was a clandestine warning of some kind...

How would Mr. Leto know that she worked for the agency? They had never discussed her work and, to her knowledge, he had never followed her to the building where she worked. His injured leg barely allowed him to walk around his tiny bookstore.

Or was that an act?

Anxiety seized her and she thought he could be another spy.

Perhaps he was a contact trying to warn her about the upcoming assignment. Even if the warning were friendly, how did anyone outside of the agency know what she was doing? No one beyond a few men on the fifth floor knew what she was doing.

And there was a matter of timing. The last time she was able to break free and visit the bookstore was a week ago. That was before she'd been given the assignment. It couldn't be old Mr. Leto.

Was someone from the inside trying to throw her off track? Trying to make her more insecure than she already was?

· · ·

WITH VARIOUS PLOTS swimming in her head, she barely glanced over when Lorraine left, still chattering about her hair. Phyllis briefly envied Lorraine. All she had to think about was the wedding. Phyllis had too much on her mind and it was giving her a headache.

She decided since the note could be worrisome, she wouldn't think about it. Without knowing the sender or what the message meant, it was of little use to her.

Over dinner, Phyllis finally struck up the courage to tell Joe what was happening. Well, a semblance of the truth.

"You've cooked all this week, honey. Let me make my world-famous spaghetti tomorrow."

She had to smile. "Spaghetti is all you can cook, Joe."

"Yes, but it's known among our friends for that sauce I create."

"You do use some extraordinary ingredients." She bit her lip to suppress a laugh. "But mint and coconut? They, ah, don't seem to belong in tomato sauce."

Joe blushed. "Okay. The coconut didn't work out, but the mint gave the sauce a unique flavor."

"That much is true."

"So, I'll cook tomorrow."

Now seemed to be the time to tell him.

"You're going to be doing a lot of your own cooking for a while, honey."

The fork he raised to his mouth stopped. His wary eyes slid to hers. He put down the fork.

"Tell me."

Phyllis took a deep breath. "I'm being sent to Oak Ridge, Tennessee soon."

"Oak Ridge?"

She nodded. "That's right."

"For the agency?"

"Yes."

"To do what?"

"Secretarial work."

She could read it in his eyes that he didn't buy her explanation.

"Where precisely will you be posted?"

"The Oak Ridge National Laboratory."

His eyebrows inched toward his hairline.

"The nuclear facility?"

"Yes."

"Where scientists are conducting nuclear experiments?"

"Among other things."

He looked at her carefully. "And your expertise as a secretary is crucially needed at this time and in another state?"

"Apparently so."

"When did all this happen?"

"Last week."

"Last week," he repeated. She knew he was wondering why she was only mentioning it now. "Is it a permanent assignment?"

"No. It's only for a month."

Joe Schneider was no dummy. She knew his brain had kicked into gear. He knew she was being assigned as an agent, and at a nuclear facility. His head was probably spinning with the possibilities of what she might really be doing.

But he didn't ask.

"So, when do you leave?"

"In a few weeks."

Finally, he smiled. "Well, I guess I better learn to make something other than spaghetti."

Phyllis smiled back at him. So much was unsaid. So much *had* to be left unsaid. She really couldn't be married to anyone other than another spy. Her marriage could have ended here and now, had Joe not tacitly understood what she was saying...what she wasn't saying. Maybe one day she could tell him.

Dinner progressed with no further discussion about her transfer to Tennessee. Joe accepted her feeble explanation and continued to eat as if nothing was bothering him. He stole several glances at her plate, however. Picking up their plates to wash, he asked the question.

"You hardly touched your supper. You didn't like the stroganoff? I thought it was great."

Phyllis didn't look up. She kept her head down as she cleaned off the table, stacking silverware by the plates in the sink to be washed. "No, it was fine."

His brows scrunched together in thought. "Why didn't you eat much of it then?"

She shrugged. "Guess I wasn't too hungry."

Joe grabbed her hand as she started to walk away. "Phyllis? Honey? You never told me about your doctor appointment on Wednesday. Are you all right?"

Her eyes didn't meet his. "Yes, I'm fine."

"You and the stroganoff, huh?" he kidded.

She still didn't look at him. He tilted her chin so she had to face him.

"I can take the secrecy about going to Oak Ridge, but you can't keep a health secret from me. What's going on, sweetheart?"

Her lips quivered as she jerked her chin away. "I don't want to get into this now."

His eyes widened with alarm. "Oh no, you don't." Joe pulled Phyllis into his arms. "You're not getting away with this one. Spill it."

"Oh, Joe!" Phyllis' eyes misted with tears that spilled down her cheeks.

"You can't tell me?"

"No."

"Is the news that horrible?"

"Well..."

He wiped away her tears. "Can you write it instead?"

She smiled at him. "You always make me feel better, don't you?"

"That's my job as your husband: to make you laugh. If you can't laugh, you can at least smile."

When she didn't respond, he tried again. "Want me to get you something to write on?"

After a pause, she nodded.

"Okay."

Joe reached into a drawer to pull out a pad and a pencil. Handing them to her, he watched her carefully. She turned to scratch a few words on the pad, ripped off the small sheet and turned back to him with the paper clutched behind her.

"Am I supposed to guess? Are we playing charades?"

With tears still glistening, she shook her head. "This is no game, Joe."

"I know," he said. "It's life and it's our life. Yours and mine." He paused to watch her. "If there's a problem with one of us, the other should know. It's our jobs as husband and wife to help one another. No matter what."

"No matter what," she whispered.

"Yes."

"Promise?" She spoke so softly, he leaned forward to hear her.

"Pardon? I can't hear you."

"Do you promise?"

He crossed his heart with an extravagant motion. "Absolutely. I would never lie to you, honey."

With worry in her eyes, she slowly handed the small piece of paper to him. "Here."

Joe looked down at the few words she had scribbled. Then he glanced up.

"Remember your promise, Joe Schneider."

A wide grin split his happy face in two. The sun seemed to burst through the kitchen window enveloping Joe and Phyllis in an ethereal glow. He pulled her to him. Their eyes locked with a laser grip.

"You're pregnant?"

"It would appear so."

"Oh, honey." Joe kissed her sweetly, then more passionately as they clung to one another.

"What do you think?" she asked tentatively.

"What do I think?" He grinned, kept her close. "I think it's the most wonderful news I've heard in a long time."

"Even at a time like this?"

"At any time, this would be wonderful!"

"So, you're really happy?"

He stroked her cheek softly. "I couldn't be happier. You've made me the happiest man on the planet."

Her small smile was tentative. "That takes in a lot of territory."

"It's worth every inch."

They stood in the bright kitchen, arms around each other, staring into bright eyes. She watched dreamily until something flickered on his face.

"What?"

He shook his head. "It's nothing."

"No, it's something. Tell me what you're thinking."

The look he gave her was telling. He stepped back.

"You don't need to tell me, Phyllis, but I know the agency is sending you on assignment. We don't talk about these things, but we both know the score."

Phyllis said nothing.

"As ecstatic as I am about the baby, now I'm worried. Worried stiff. Maybe you should decline this assignment, honey."

"Decline?"

"How far along are you?"

"Just a few weeks."

"It's a critical time, Phyllis. You can't afford to do anything foolish right now."

"I won't be doing anything foolish."

"Or dangerous."

Again, she said nothing.

"Let someone else take it."

She stepped away from him. "Someone else? You know how long I've waited for an assignment, Joe! George Martin hasn't wanted to give me anything much to do, but I got an assignment anyway! I can't give it up. I can't!"

"Phyllis, another one will come along. Now isn't the time."

She turned her back to him, unwilling to let him see her tears. He had no idea how much she wanted this assignment. Watching the secondhand tick on the wall clock, her stomach fluttered, reminding her of the life she carried inside. It might have been imaginary, but Phyllis suddenly realized how much she wanted this baby.

Maybe Joe was right.

He pulled her back to him. "Why don't we sleep on it? Discuss it again in the morning."

She leaned into him, grateful for his strength. "It's a deal. I'm wiped out."

Joe brought her hand up to his lips for a kiss. "Come on, Mrs. Schneider. Tonight, you're all mine and tomorrow..."

"Tomorrow is another day."

"That's right."

As he led her to the bedroom, Phyllis shook the unwanted thoughts from her head.

Tomorrow.

She'd think about it tomorrow.

DON'T DO IT.

Phyllis awoke the next morning with the small phrase echoing in her mind. *Don't do it.*It must relate to her assignment in Tennessee. Nothing else made sense.

Joe had been called for an early emergency meeting of his department. They hadn't been able to continue last night's discussion, but that was all right. Maybe it was best to let last night simmer.

She went about her day in a light state of dread as *Don't do it* was never far from her thoughts. A quick doctor appointment at lunch lulled her into a quasi-sense of security. She'd gone to see him again to allay her fears about going on assignment early in her pregnancy. Her doctor informed her that going to Tennessee for a month shouldn't be a problem. She would be back in Washington for the second trimester. The news settled her down so she could concentrate on the task at hand.

She reasoned she would hardly be gone at all. Major Simpson told her at the meeting this afternoon that her relocation was moved up timewise for security reasons. She was leaving in eight days now and would be at Oak Ridge for four short weeks.

Her stomach fluttered again at the thought of leaving Joe so soon. They'd be fine.

Joe wasn't so sure. He didn't say much when she told him, but his eyes gave him away. His anxiety wasn't disguised, even for the experienced agent he was.

That Sunday, Joe and Phyllis went to her sister's house for dinner. Connie and Jeff Wallace, plus their two lively children, lived a few blocks away from Phyllis and Joe. A fact that seemed to work its way into every conversation.

"I swear, Phyllis. We saw more of you when you lived in Norway than we do now." The elfish pout on Connie's face seemed childlike with her short pixie haircut.

Phyllis refrained from rolling her eyes. "Can we not start this again?"

Del Bowden, Connie and Phyllis' father, had no such qualms. His eyes flew to the ceiling, followed by a snort aimed at Joe and Jeff.

"They were always at it as kids. I see times haven't changed."

"Well, it's true, Dad," insisted Connie. "They only live two blocks from here."

"Perhaps they have a lot going on, hon," said Jeff. "Give them a break."

"What could they possibly have going on?" Connie scoffed before standing to clear the table.

Phyllis shot a glance at Joe. She'd managed to steer the conversation away from topics she wasn't prepared to talk about...like the pregnancy and her job in Tennessee. Joe's return look was one of relief.

She helped her sister with the dishes, as Joe helped Del into an armchair in the living room. The kids listened to the radio, and the music had lulled Del to sleep before Joe left the room.

"Your dad's asleep already," he told Phyllis and Connie back in the kitchen.

Connie nodded. "He tires so easily these days."

"Can you tell me more about his latest doctor visit?" asked Phyllis.

"Sure." Connie ran warm water to wash dishes. Phyllis picked up a towel to dry. Joe stood off to one side, while Jeff went to check on the kids.

"He seems so pale."

"The new medications are tough on his system, the doctor told me, and he's not tolerating them well." Connie looked at her sister. "He's sick a lot, so I've practically moved him into our guest room. I don't want him in that big old house by himself."

"Seems reasonable. What can I do to help?"

Connie reached a wet hand out to Phyllis. "You don't understand. The cancer is getting worse."

Phyllis shivered with her touch and the news. "Worse? You don't mean that he's..." She couldn't bring herself to say it.

Joe stepped close to lay his hand on her shoulder.

"It's hard to tell the future, sis. We've got to just hang in there and keep him as comfortable as possible."

"Want me to bring him to our house a few days a week?"

Connie shook her head. "He's fine here. Too much movement isn't good for him. His balance is shaky too."

"Well, what else can I do?"

As the sisters continued to discuss how to handle their father's health crisis, Joe and Jeff exchanged a knowing look.

Joe cleared his throat.

"May I make a suggestion?"

"Sure, Joe," said Connie. "Go ahead."

"All the activities you are proposing are fine, but there's something else you can do."

"What's that, honey?" asked Phyllis. She'd finished drying the final dish and laid the towel on the counter.

"You need to make arrangements for the...future."

"That's what we're doing, aren't we?" Connie dried her hands and looked over at Joe.

"I don't think Joe means those kinds of arrangements, Connie."

"Well, for heaven's sake, Jeff. What other kind of arrangements could he mean?" The longer she looked at Joe, the wider her eyes became. She finally got his meaning.

"You mean funeral arrangements."

"Oh, Joe. Really?" Phyllis began to wring her hands. "Must we?"

"It's too soon," added Connie.

"It's not too soon," said Jeff with feeling. "You girls have put this off, but while your dad is still of sound mind, you need to get his will in order. What does he want to leave to whom and all that."

Joe took ahold of Phyllis' hands. "Honey, you and your sister need to do this."

She swallowed hard, but the lump in her throat wouldn't go down.

"You and Connie talk a bit more. Jeff and I will join the kids."

When the men left, Connie hugged her sister. "Has it come to this?"

"Apparently so. Will Dad mind?"

"Maybe he already has a will. I've never asked him."

"I guess we should do that."

"Okay." Connie thought a minute. "Could we get together next week to decide what all to ask him?"

"Next week?" Phyllis ran through her mental calendar. "I'm preparing for the Tennessee trip, but maybe I can squeeze this in."

Connie's brows furrowed. "You're going to Tennessee?"

"Um, yes, for work."

"You're a secretary at the State Department. What could you possibly need to go to Tennessee for?"

Phyllis licked her lips. She wasn't allowed to tell friends or family about working for the CIA, thus Connie's remark about the State Department. And this was precisely why she hadn't wanted to tell her sister too much.

Connie's hands flew up. "Okay, okay. Don't tell me, but when will you be back?"

"In a month."

"A month?" Her mouth dropped open. "Why in the world would you need to stay a month? Is this a promotion?"

"Sort of."

"That makes no sense, Phyllis Bowden Schneider. Explain in concise terms please."

Phyllis shook her head. "That's really all I can say, Connie."

Col. Lawrence's words about having to explain to loved ones came back to her in a rush.

"You've barely said anything."

Connie looked hard at her sister. "I know you haven't always told me the complete story about what you do, sis. Dad told me not to ask many questions. Does he know more than I do about the jobs you've had?"

Phyllis considered her sister's question. "I think he's a better guesser than you are, Connie. That's all."

"A better guesser."

"Yeah. But maybe you could get started on his directives while I'm away. I'll call the minute I'm back."

"You really can't meet me this week?"

"It doesn't look good."

In the car on the way home, Phyllis turned to Joe.

"I hate not being able to tell my family what I do for a living. It seems so dishonest to have to lie or tell half-truths to Connie."

"What about your dad?"

"I suspect he knows. Remember when I returned home to Washington after Oslo?"

"Yes."

"We had a confidential chat without Connie present."

"What did you tell him?"

"Not much. He told me that he was proud of the job I was doing and to be careful because he knew it was probably dangerous."

"You didn't mention anything about me?"

"I mentioned your involvement with finding out who had double-crossed Col. Lawrence in London. Dad must have put two and two together about us both."

Joe smiled. "Smart man, your dad."

"He's the best."

For the next few minutes, the scene Phyllis had described to Joe flashed through her mind. She and her father had stayed up late one night. She'd gone to his house to check on him.

Del Bowden had been a mining geologist. He was a professional through and through. His job took him to international locations and exotic settings. Work in the field kept his mind occupied with all manner of geologic study. He could collect samples to observe the fabric within the rocks. He could analyze the data from the samples to get a better view of what substances could be forthcoming: gold, silver, lithium and copper, to name a few. Although various illnesses in his life had felled his career, Del Bowden was still as sharp as they come. Now gray-haired and slumped, the man could still read his daughter.

"How was Oslo?"

Phyllis had shrugged. What to say? "Not that interesting. You would have been bored."

Del laughed. "Hardly! You work in a country that was just liberated after five years of occupation by the Germans, and you call that boring?"

Phyllis smiled. Of course, her father would catch that. "The work was boring, Dad, not the country."

"You must have seen some interesting things. There was a purge going on, as I recall."

Images of women with shaved heads and swastikas drawn on their foreheads immediately came to mind.

"And I heard the children had a rough time too."

A picture of a sweet little girl Phyllis had rescued came to view but was washed away with tears.

Del touched her arm. "You're crying, daughter. Why?"

She took a deep breath. "I saw and experienced more than I can ever tell you about." Her head sank to her chest.

"Phyllis. Honey. Look at me. I'm not as dumb as I look."

She shook her head, wiping away the tears. "I never said you were!"

"Let me summarize your career since you won't do it for me." A grin amidst his wrinkles did much to lighten the mood. "You worked as a secretary in the Justice Department here in Washington DC. You must have met influential people because, before Connie and I knew it, you were on a plane to London eight months before the war was over. Why would you go over at that time?"

He shook his head at her. "No, don't say anything."

Phyllis had smiled. This was so like her father to figure everything out before she could say a word. He should have been a detective.

"In London, your boss, the Military Attaché at the Embassy, gets arrested for espionage. Somehow, you find out what happened and the people responsible." His grin widened across his thin face. "I can't believe investigation of war crimes was in your job description."

"Dad..."

He held up a hand. "And you meet Joe Schneider over there. He helps you clear your boss of espionage charges and he works for the State Department too. I would have liked being in on his job interview as well."

"Um, well, he..."

"No." He chuckled at her discomfort. "Not done yet."

She squirmed in her chair.

"Then you're transferred to Oslo, Norway mere months after the Germans leave. You were probably one of the first American women to arrive in that country. You stay a year, working for military officers at the War Department, so you say, and rescue a little girl."

Her lips parted in surprise.

"You gave yourself away, sweetie. I know you helped some little child while you were there." He held up his hand. "You come home with Joe, after having gotten married onboard ship in the North Sea. He looks like he's been chewed up and spit out. You never said what happened to him, and you don't have to. I know you both had important jobs in the war."

Del took a sip of water and handed her the glass.

"Dad..."

"Sweetie, it doesn't take a mining geologist to figure out you and Joe are in military intelligence. Being English, he was probably MI5, right?"

"You know I can't say."

"I bet you were OSS overseas. Are you in the CIA now?"

All her tradecraft training couldn't save her from the acknowledgment that flashed on her face.

"Thought so."

"Dad, I work for the State Department."

"Sure you do. What department?"

"Apple imports."

The sound of Del Bowden's laughter echoed in her ears.

Joe reached over to stroke her arm, intruding on the memory. "You with me?"

"Sure. I was just remembering Dad."

"You and Connie will get this sorted out."

"I hope so and before it's too late."

Even as she said the words, Phyllis knew the clock was ticking. Ticking about many things besides her dear father.

THREE

JOE

Phyllis had left for Tennessee yesterday. She hadn't wanted to fly, but putting her on that train was one of the hardest things he'd done in years.

She hasn't been in the field for some time. Even then Col. Lawrence closely monitored her while she was stationed in Norway. Lawrence insisted she keep in close touch and called for more security when the situation warranted it.

But this was different.

Vastly different.

She was on assignment far away from Washington. He had no idea if the agency had assigned back-up for her, but he knew security precautions were always built into every assignment. He also knew, from personal experience, that sometimes those precautions could backfire or disappear as the situation changed. Every assignment was an exercise in flexibility for the field agent.

Just ask Mata Hari, the exotic dancer who was

convicted of being a spy for Germany during World War I.

The thought caused him to smile, just a little bit, before lapsing back into his perpetual frown.

Phyllis probably hadn't told her handler that she was pregnant. He wasn't sure what the protocol was for pregnant agents, but he bet they were sidelined, at least for the duration of the pregnancy and some months after. Maybe he could covertly find out those regulations.

And who was her handler? He knew many of the upper management within the CIA, due to the position he held and his high security clearance. These days he trained agents for work in the field as to logistics, transportation and weaponry.

Her handler could not be the unpopular George Martin, Phyllis' current boss. He'd learned just this morning from a rumor he heard at the water cooler that Martin was set to be transferred to a lesser position of authority within the month, simply because he was ineffective. Martin had no people skills and could hardly keep up with his workload. If it weren't for his soon-to-be-promoted secretary, Martin would have been out of a job a year ago.

So, Phyllis was on her own in unknown territory with their future child. The mere thought had him restless and twitching. He stretched his long legs under his desk to get some respite. It didn't work.

"Schneider! What the hell are you frowning about?"

Mitch Ender, agent in the next cubicle over, leaned back in his chair. Any further and he'd be lying on the floor with that goofy smirk on his face. Serve him right.

"What?"

"You look like your grandmother just died. What's the news?"

"My grandmother is alive and well, thank you, Ender. What's it to you?"

Joe hadn't meant to snap at the guy, but it came out that way.

"Criminy. Don't snap my head off. I was just makin' polite conversation."

Joe shook his head. It didn't make him forget about Phyllis, but it might help him get back to work.

"Sorry, Mitch. Got a lot on my mind."

"Like what?"

"Huh?"

"What's got you tied up in knots? Your wife throw you out or something?"

Joe glanced around the spacious room filled with people, noise and fluttering paper. For the moment, he couldn't remember what report he was writing.

"Joe."

"What?"

"You don't look so good. Want to grab some lunch?"

"It's not lunch time."

"Look at your watch."

Joe turned his wrist to check his watch.

"One o'clock."

"You're right, Schneider. It's not lunchtime; it's after lunchtime. Let's go. You need a break."

"Let me just finish..."

"Nope. No can do. Come on." With that, Mitch sprang off his chair and unfurled all six feet four inches over Joe sitting at his desk.

"Well, if you're going to throw your weight around."

"Let's hit it. I need a beer."

"At lunch?"

Mitch laughed. "You're right. We both need a beer. Let's go."

A smile cracked Joe's face. He closed the file he was working on and slid it into a drawer. After locking it, he stood by Mitch. With an exaggerated motion, Mitch swept his arm towards the door.

"After you, my kind sir. Your carriage awaits."

Joe laughed. "Who are you? Sir Walter Raleigh?"

"Just so, my good man. Just so."

FOUR

PHYLLIS

Phyllis didn't know what made her glance over her left shoulder and she wasn't happy when she did.

The train was packed with travelers bundled to the max. Thick coats, woolen scarves and hats were in abundance. The weather had worsened in the past week sending temperatures to lower digits and lightly dressed people to their hall closets for warmer outerwear.

A man towards the rear of her train car caught her attention, mainly because he was trying not to. A newspaper covered his face up to his nose, but his eyes were checking out the room. After a thorough inspection of the immediate vicinity, the man's gaze fell upon Phyllis. When he realized she was watching him, the newspaper rose significantly to cover all but the top of his head.

Phyllis noted his thinning gray hair and a silver ring on his left hand. His fingers were neatly manicured and glints from sunshine through the train window reflected off the shiny ring.

She turned her attention out the window to watch the changing landscape. Riding the train from Washington to Tennessee hadn't even been a choice. She detested air travel after having flown on cargo planes to England and Norway. The planes were huge and clunky, and seemed to hit every air pocket in the sky. With her stomach already queasy, she didn't want to take any chances of getting sick. Also, Phyllis couldn't imagine that commercial flights were much better than the planes used by the military, so she refused to fly on one. Joe always grinned like an idiot when they discussed it, but she wasn't changing her mind. A train was on the ground where the people were. Birds belonged in the sky.

The landscape traveling through Virginia and on into Tennessee didn't change very much. Lots of wooded areas and farms with the occasional city. Keeping one eye on the stranger in the rear, Phyllis yawned and stretched. It was nearing noon and she was hungry. She rose to walk to the club car to get some lunch.

Before she stepped from her row, the suspicious man appeared in the aisle. He smiled benignly in her direction and started to walk past when a book dropped out of his hand. It thudded loudly when it hit the train floor, causing Phyllis to take a step back.

"Sorry, miss. Didn't mean to scare you."

"I'm fine, thank you."

When he bent down to retrieve the fallen book, Phyllis saw the outline of a gun in his coat pocket. She took another step back.

He looked at the book she was holding.

"That's an interesting story. Have you read much of Camus' work?"

"No, this is the first."

"I think you'll find his work enlightening."

"I'm sure I will." *Enlightening*? Where had she heard that before?

He made no motion to leave.

"Albert Camus was a French citizen who joined the resistance during the war."

"Fascinating. Now if you will excuse me."

"But he opposed the Soviet Union. Not a wise move, in my estimation."

Phyllis stared at him. His heavy accent indicated he was from another country, possibly Russia. Several fingers of his left hand were in his pocket close to the gun. The finger with the shiny silver ring stayed out. A large mole on his right cheek seemed to have a life of its own. Phyllis noted his tiny chin and bushy mustache before deciding to focus on the silver ring. It didn't seem as sinister as the rest of him. Up close, an intricate design etched in the silver seemed to resemble a bear.

"I really must go." When she stepped into the aisle, the man blocked her path to the exit.

"I must speak with you, Miss Bowden."

Her lips parted slightly in surprise that he knew her name. Her maiden name at that.

"How do you know me?"

"We know many things about you."

"What do you want?"

"It is of paramount importance to my government that you hear me out, as you Americans say."

He looked toward the exit.

"You were heading to the club car?"

"Yes."

"Please let me join you. I could use some refreshment also. Allow me to buy you lunch."

Her hand waved him off. "That's not necessary."

"But it is to me." His dark eyes beseeched her. "Please? Just a short chat over a bowl of soup?"

Her eyes met his. "Will you keep that gun in your pocket and not aim it at me?" She patted her purse. "I have one too."

"I suspected. Yes, I will be the perfect gentleman." He motioned toward the exit door to the next car. "After you."

Phyllis shot him a last wary look before walking toward the door. She'd have to telegraph this to the agency. She had already guessed that he was a foreign agent, but what he wanted, she had no clue. She knew what she had to do.

She pushed the train car door open with renewed confidence and took a step into the club car. Phyllis heard soft footsteps behind her. The dining area was too public a place for any hostile confrontation, which made her wonder all the more what exactly the man wanted.

She soon found out.

FIVE

JOE

Mitch Ender's deep baritone echoed in the restaurant. A few people glanced over to see who was making the noise.

"Lower your voice, Mitch," said Joe. He'd lived his life trying not to call attention to himself and Ender was beginning to irritate him.

Mitch laughed, a deep booming sound. "Just enjoying my lunch, Schneider. You're so grouchy today."

"I'm not grouchy, just sensitive to loud noises."

"Oh, sorry," whispered Mitch. "How's this level?"

Mitch's impish attitude made Joe grin despite his grouchy mood.

"That's better. You're lookin' human."

Joe drank his coffee. "Man, this is better than I make."

"Tired of your cookin'?"

"I'll say. I was never any good at it." Joe smiled. "All those ingredients in a recipe. Never could figure out what went in first, second or third. I get them all muddled and make a mess, instead of a good roast with potatoes."

"When is your wife back from her trip?" Joe had explained to anyone who asked that Phyllis was visiting relatives.

"A few days."

"Maybe you could come over to my house for dinner one night so you won't starve. My wife is a great cook." He laughed again, holding on to his ample stomach. "As you can see for yourself."

Mitch Ender was easy to like. He didn't bother people, generally, and was a good agent. His fieldwork had ended, like Joe's, but he liked his desk job and was happy with his work.

Just as Mitch signaled the waiter for the check, several things happened at once.

A small child sitting at a table nearby started crying at the top of his voice. His mother and father couldn't quiet him and they rose to pluck him out of his chair. Moving quickly, the mother stepped in front of a waiter carrying a tray filled with food to deliver. The waiter lost his footing when he tried to move away from her and dumped the whole tray, dishes with steaming hot food and glasses filled with water, at the foot of Joe and Mitch's table.

Beads of perspiration broke out on Joe's face as his mind raced to comprehend what had happened. He grabbed onto the table for support.

"Hey!" yelled Mitch just as black dots began to cloud Joe's vision. Before Mitch could catch him, Joe slipped out of his chair in a dead faint, right into plates of mashed potatoes, meat loaf, hamburgers and fruit salad.

SIX

THE TRAIN RIDE

The older man looked at Phyllis over his menu.

"Tomato soup with a grilled cheese sandwich looks good. What do you think?" When he smiled, the mole on his left cheek twitched. Phyllis glanced away to other customers in the train club car.

"Pretty good. I was thinking of having that myself."

"Fine. That's settled then." The man laid his menu on the edge of the table. A young waiter in a dark uniform stepped over smartly to pick it up. He looked from the man to Phyllis.

"Are you ready to order?"

"Yes," said the man. "We both would like the tomato soup with grilled cheese." He looked up at the waiter. "Is the soup fresh?"

"Yes, sir."

When the man nodded, the young waiter clicked the top of his pen in his response.

After he had left, the man caught Phyllis' wandering gaze.

"Miss Bowden."

"Mrs. Schneider."

"Ah, yes." His lopsided smile revealed straight teeth, slightly yellow. Several fingers were stained with nicotine.

"Do you mind if I smoke?"

"I do, actually."

"All right." He tucked a small package of cigarettes back into a pocket.

"Who are you?"

"My name is of no importance."

Phyllis shook her head. "That's not true. Your name is very important."

He nodded. "Jeremy Smith."

A giggle nearly bubbled out of her. "You don't look like a Jeremy Smith."

"I hear that all the time."

She shook her head again. "This conversation is over if I don't hear truth from you."

"All right. My name is Igor Ivanov."

A smile on her face replaced the giggle. "Why did you lie just then?"

"I didn't." He held up his hands in defense. "Jeremy Smith is the name I usually use because Igor Ivanov gets no respect."

"You're looking for respect?"

"I'm looking to blend in."

She shrugged her shoulders. "You might have trouble doing that with your accent. It does mark you as someone from another country."

The waiter chose that moment to set a bowl of soup in front of Phyllis. After Igor had received his, the waiter nodded and left.

He blew on a spoonful of soup before swallowing.

"Good. It's very good." He nodded to her. "Go on. You must be hungry."

"Why must I be hungry?"

"Because it's lunchtime and you've had a long trip so far, coming from Washington, D.C."

Phyllis maintained a neutral face, but was again surprised. She swallowed tomato soup instead of responding.

"Is it to your satisfaction?"

"Yes." Phyllis put down her spoon. "Before we sit here a minute longer, I want to know what you want."

"Of course. You Americans always rush to the point."

"And?"

Igor calmly spooned another bite of soup. "It really is delicious."

Phyllis stared at him.

"We know who you are, Mrs. Schneider." He lowered his voice. "Your assignment is fruitless because we are onto you. You will not succeed."

"Who are you, Igor Ivanov?"

"A friend."

"Are you NKGB? Are you Secret Police?"

He pursed his lips. "Let's say that my people have an interest in the man you are seeking. The deck, as you say, is stacked against you in this matter and you will not be successful."

"How do you know what I'm seeking?"

Igor leaned closer. "You are seeking the engineer who has evidence against a certain British scientist giving information to the Soviets." He angled his head. "Is that not correct?"

"And if it were." Phyllis narrowed her eyes. "You

are the last person I would admit it to."

He chuckled, dipped his spoon into the steaming soup.

"We've heard you are very good, Mrs. Schneider, which is why I have a proposition for you."

"I'm listening."

"Please eat your soup. It will get cold."

She picked up her spoon for another bite.

"We would like you to work for us."

"Work for you?"

"Yes."

Phyllis laughed. "I don't even know who you are."

"But we know who you are," he countered. "You received a note in an Albert Camus book recently, did you not?"

Her eyes widened. "What note?"

"I'm sure you remember a note that fell out of your book on the streetcar."

"You've been following me."

"Yes, but not for the reason you think."

"And what reason would that be?"

He smiled. "Let's move on to the purpose of the note."

"The note came from you? Does Mr. Leto at the bookstore work for you?"

"We occasionally have common interests."

"You must be a Russian agent."

"Why must I be?"

"And Mr. Leto is also NKGB?"

"Alas, he is not."

Phyllis kept a neutral face.

"Who I work for is of no importance."

When Phyllis put down her spoon and crossed her

arms across her chest, Igor hesitated.

"All right. Let me speak plainly. My appearance may be deceptive, because I work for British intelligence."

"I find that hard to believe."

"You may believe what you choose to."

Phyllis turned her spoon over to study the detail on the back.

"I assume you have contacted me for a reason."

"Yes."

"You want me to do something for you?"

"We would like you to turn the engineer over to us when you capture him."

"I thought you said I would be unsuccessful."

"We can help if you help us."

"And his wife?"

"We have no interest in his wife. You may take her with you."

"Why do you want him?"

The agent blinked with wide eyes. "I thought it would be obvious. We don't want him to expose the scientist."

"Why would the British want to keep a traitor in place?"

"He is not giving good information. He has been feeding the Soviets phony information. We want him to continue his job of disinformation."

Phyllis mulled that over. His announcement was confusing. On one hand, he appeared to be Russian. Yet, he said he worked for British intelligence and wanted the spy to continue spreading false information to the Soviets. Something didn't add up.

"How do I know this is the truth?"

"Why would I lie?"

She laughed. "I can think of many reasons."

He looked honestly confused. "Like what?"

"That I might be successful and the British scientist goes to jail for selling atomic secrets."

"Going to jail would not be good for our cause." He tugged at his sleeve. "We are prepared to offer you a great deal of money for your assistance."

Before she could dismiss Igor's money offer, the waiter brought the grilled cheese sandwiches.

"Are you finished with your soup?"

"Yes," replied Phyllis. Her appetite had waned while chatting with this man. "Please take my bowl."

"Wasn't it to your liking?"

"Thank you, yes. I'm just ready for the sandwich."

The waiter glanced from Phyllis to Igor, set down the plates, took their bowls and left quietly.

Phyllis picked up her sandwich. Before taking a bite, she nodded to Igor.

"I'll think about it. How can I get in contact with you?"

His face showed no expression. He pulled a business card from his pocket.

"Here is my number. Please call me any hour of the day or night."

"Thank you." Phyllis tucked the card in her purse, before turning her complete attention to her food. "This looks good."

The rest of the short meal ended in silence, except for sounds of the food being consumed. When she finished, Phyllis wiped her mouth with a napkin and rose.

"Thanks for lunch. I'll be in touch."

SEVEN

JOE

Bright light invaded Joe's consciousness. Somewhere words from a deep baritone voice pinged in Joe's head giving him a headache.

"So, what's wrong with him, nurse?"

"Are you a relative?"

"No. We work together."

"I'm afraid you'll have to ask the doctor."

"There aren't any doctors in sight. There's just you."

Joe's weary eyes blinked open.

"For heaven's sake, Ender. Give it a rest."

Mitch's laugh boomed in the small space. "Well, I'll be. Sleeping Beauty awakens."

"Excuse me, sir," said the young woman by Joe's bed. "You'll have to step out for a few minutes while I take his vitals."

Mitch laughed again. "Don't take his vitals, miss. His wife will get really pissed."

The nurse brought her cart alongside Joe's bed. Her blush was easily seen in the brightly lit room.

"All right. I'm going."

After taking Joe's temperature and blood pressure, he studied her serious young face.

"How am I?"

"Your doctor is making his rounds and will be in to talk to you shortly."

"Can you tell me what happened?"

"Certainly. You fainted at a restaurant and your friend brought you to this hospital."

"I fainted?"

"Yes."

He was honestly puzzled. "Can you tell me why I fainted?"

"No, sir. The doctor has that information."

He knew it was useless to press the nurse, so he closed his eyes and listened to a pair of footsteps—one pair going out of the room and another pair coming in. Joe opened his eyes to see Mitch Ender staring at him from the foot of the bed.

"You don't look any worse for wear."

"Thanks."

"You really took a nosedive into the mashed potatoes. Care to tell me what disease you've got?"

"No disease."

"Somethin' made you keel over."

"Loud noises bother me sometimes."

"That kid cryin'."

"And whatever the crash was."

"Some waiter bumped into the kid's mother and a zillion dishes crashed to the floor."

"By me?"

Mitch nodded. "Right at your feet."

"That did it then."

"Did what exactly?"

Joe hesitated. He hadn't told many people about his past experiences as an agent and didn't know how much Mitch knew.

"I, ah..."

"I know you came off bad on your last assignment, Schneider."

"Who told you that?"

"I'm a trained agent too. I can tell when a job has gone sideways."

Joe closed his eyes. "Things didn't end well for me in Romania. I've been diagnosed with battle fatigue."

"Battle fatigue?"

Joe nodded. "It comes and goes whenever it wants."

"You gettin' help?"

"Yeah."

Mitch was silent for a moment. "Your wife knows?"

"Of course."

"Huh."

Joe opened his eyes with a smile. "What? No advice from the great Mitch Ender?"

"Not off the top of my head. Sorry, man. It must have been a rough assignment."

"It wasn't good."

Joe and Mitch looked at one another. Before either could respond, the nurse came back in.

"Mr. Ender? Is that your name?"

"Yes, ma'am."

"There's a phone call for you. You can take it at the nurses' station down the hall."

Mitch smiled at Joe. "Be right back. My wife probably wants me to pick up somethin' at the store."

"Sure."

After Mitch left, a doctor came in to discuss Joe's condition. He said nothing illuminating from what Joe already knew. He dozed after the doctor left.

Heavy footsteps walked in the room.

"Schneider? You asleep?"

"I was trying."

"Gotta go, man."

Joe blinked open his eyes. "What's the rush? Gotta get those groceries?"

"No." Mitch lowered his voice. "That was work. "

"Work?"

"Yeah." He turned his head to check if anyone was behind him. "I'm going back in the field."

Joe's eyes widened. "Back in the field? Thought you were out."

Mitch shrugged. "Guess they're pulling me out of mothballs for this quick trip. Gotta help an agent in trouble."

Joe couldn't keep his eyes open. "Well, good luck and stay out of trouble yourself."

Minutes after Mitch left and right before his mind retreated into sleep, Joe wondered what agent was in trouble. He hoped it was no one he knew, but just before darkness descended, his mind shouted one word: Phyllis.

EIGHT

PHYLLIS

Phyllis was antsy. She crossed her legs. She uncrossed her legs. She had run her fingers through her curly hair so often that she finally got a comb from her purse to put her messy bobbed hair back in place.

Glancing out the window, Phyllis barely noticed the changing landscape or the constant rhythmic movement of the train. Tall poles went by with a rapid pace. Phone poles? Poles used for electricity? She neither knew nor cared.

She tried to read her book, but the author Albert Camus had too much covert meaning for her. Concentrating on the book wasn't possible. She closed it and set it on the seat next to her.

Once she looked over her shoulder and saw Igor. He looked up from the book he was reading and beamed a bright smile her way. When he waved his book in the air, Phyllis quickly looked away. One eye had developed a slight tic. Her tongue stuck to the roof of her mouth.

Phyllis couldn't wait to get off the train.

Her mind raced with bombarding thoughts. How did that man know about her assignment? How did he know about her? Who precisely did he work for?

Her stomach churned in response. Maybe there was a leak at the agency. That seemed unlikely. The fifth floor of her building was the most secretive and only those with the highest security clearances were allowed inside.

She hadn't said much to Joe, although he guessed she was being sent on assignment. She hadn't told him why she was going and he didn't ask. Being an agent himself, Joe wouldn't have asked. He was only concerned for her safety, as a good husband would be.

It bothered her that Mr. Leto, the old bookseller, must know that she worked for the CIA. Bothered her, but strangely enough didn't surprise her. He always seemed rather secretive and knowing, in an abstract sort of way.

The warning note had slipped from the book he insisted that she buy. Mr. Leto must have sent the note, but why? And how would he know about her mission? The handwriting on the note was such small script that the profession of architect popped into her mind. Her next thought was Mr. Leto had once mentioned he'd been an architect years ago, long before buying the bookstore.

That it was possible Mr. Leto knew much more than he appeared to, made her head throb. Phyllis rose from her seat to go to the club car for a glass of water. After downing an aspirin, she went back to her seat. In her condition, she thought twice about taking headache medication, but her pounding head took center stage. A glance towards the back of the train car informed her that Igor was nowhere in sight. Where'd he go?

She shook her head and sat down. It didn't matter. She was going to phone in her report as soon as she reached Oak Ridge.

Major Simpson could decide the best choice of action at this point. Phyllis felt she had handled the unsavory business with Igor the best she could. She didn't want to have the assignment terminated, but things had certainly changed. Simpson would decide her future course of action.

She closed her eyes. Her stomach still bothered her and there had been tiny drops of blood in her urine when she went to the bathroom.

Phyllis drifted into an uneasy sleep.

NINE

MAJOR SIMPSON

Dick Simpson replaced the phone gently in its cradle and stared unseeing out the window.

Unbelievable.

Phyllis' news was simply unbelievable.

Security for this assignment had been locked up tight. Only a few people knew about it and those few he worked with every day. How was it possible that a British intelligence agent not only knew what Phyllis was going to do, but had the nerve to bribe her into becoming a double agent?

Simply unbelievable.

What to do about it?

His first reaction was to give lie detector tests to all those he worked with on a daily basis. Someone had leaked the information. His reaction wasn't knee-jerk. It followed protocol, and he had to act quickly. Phyllis had arrived in Oak Ridge and would be reporting for duty at the nuclear facility in the morning. He had to do something now.

Phyllis mentioned the agent had a Russian name

and accent, but identified himself as British. That information muddied the waters. Not only was his identity confusing, but so was the reason why the man didn't want her assignment to be successful. He told her the British scientist was feeding the Soviets misinformation. If that were true, why hadn't Simpson heard about it? He had the latest intelligence reports and nothing had brought up the idea the spy was purposely misleading the Soviets. And why would the British want this done? Whose brainchild was it to feed bad information to the Soviets? He needed answers.

No. Simpson mulled it over and came up with the conclusion that the whole thing was bogus. Of course the scientist was feeding the Soviets correct information. The CIA had solid evidence of his betrayal. The Soviets obviously wanted Phyllis to deliver the whistleblower to them.

One thing was perfectly clear—Phyllis' cover was blown. If Ivanov was Russian Secret Police, which he most certainly had to be, then Phyllis was in trouble.

Simpson knew he should pull her out of the assignment and abort the mission. But he couldn't do it by phone. He needed to send someone to inform her in person.

Who?

Major Simpson didn't trust any of the people around him on the fifth floor. Not now. He would need to reach out to someone no one would expect. Someone who had been out of the field for a while.

He spent the better part of the next hour going through lists of retired agents. When he read Joe Scheider's name, Simpson got an idea. Of course, he couldn't use Joe, but who was the man in the next cubicle next to Joe?

Bender, Sender, Render. His eyes skimmed the paper in his hand.

Ender. That was it. Mitch Ender.

The man had been an excellent field agent, but had requested a desk job when he got married two years ago. Making a few calls, Simpson finally located Mitch at the hospital. He learned Joe Schneider had had an episode and that Ender had taken him to a local hospital.

His call to Mitch Ender was terse and brief.

"Mitch? Dick Simpson here."

"Major. To what do I owe the honor?"

"How's Joe doing?"

"He's all right."

"Do you know when he'll be released?"

"Today, I think. You tracked me down about Joe?"

Simpson phrased his words carefully.

"No, although I'm sorry to hear about his accident. Ender, this isn't a secure line, so I want you to come up to the fifth floor once you leave the hospital."

The request left Mitch momentarily stunned. "The fifth, you say? Um, well, all right, sir."

"The only thing I can say is that I need your help."

"Yes, sir."

"You might be able to help out a friend in need."

"A friend, sir?"

"Nothing further on this line, Ender. Please report in as soon as you can."

When he hung up the phone, Dick Simpson leaned back into the thick cushions of his chair. Looking around the office at various plaques and pictures, souvenirs of success, he vowed this assignment wasn't going to go haywire. With Ender's help, the mission would go off as expected. The engineer would be extracted and the British spy would be caught.

Success was paramount to the country's well-being. Failure was not an option.

Major Simpson sent out the order for everyone on the fifth floor to report for lie detector testing.

TEN

THE TARGET

Peter Gresham looked around his office at the Oak Ridge National Laboratory. He was tucked into one of the buildings near the road leading out of the complex. His office wasn't in a good location and he knew his abilities were being overlooked. But that's the way it had always been.

A family picture caught his eye. A tall, white-haired man stood next to a smallish woman with a panicked look on her face. His mother always looked like someone, her husband generally, was about to scold her. Peter had spent a good part of his childhood coming to her rescue, much to the resentment of his father.

A decent likeness of Peter in his early twenties resembled the taller man next to him—his brother, Graham. Dr. Graham Gresham, if you please.

And he didn't. Peter had never liked his brother much, mainly because their father made it a point to showcase Graham's brilliant scientific mind at every opportunity. It was always Graham did this and

Graham invented that. Graham was the star of the family and everyone had to acquiesce to his bidding.

His bidding was constant and relentless. As younger brother, Peter was forced to tag along with Graham, in case he needed anything. Basically, what Graham seemed to need the most was someone to rescue him whenever he got in trouble, which was often.

Graham Gresham had been taught that the world was his oyster to do with as he pleased. He did his utmost to make sure the world knew it, and his haughty attitude made him unpopular.

Peter played catch-up and when Graham's trouble got too hot, Peter had to sort it out. After twenty years of helping his brother, Peter had had enough. His level of resentment was as high as his office ceiling. He grabbed the family picture, opened a desk drawer and tossed it in. Hearing glass break, Peter shut the drawer again only harder. He'd come to a breaking point, like the glass in the picture frame.

Glancing out a tiny window by his desk in the cramped office, Peter wondered why he'd let things get so far out of control. Yes, his father had always been demanding. Yes, his mother always needed to be else- where, so she could stay out of the line of fire. Her participation in a number of charities and other phil- anthropic institutions was long.

He and Graham were only a year apart, so they'd gone to university together. Graham's brilliance got him into Oxford and their father's connections and money got Peter in as well. Peter had to go with his brother to keep him in line, of course. That was his duty in the family.

During their university years, Graham's star shined brighter and brighter. He truly had a brilliant scientific mind in the area of molecular physics. He understood the world in terms that no one around him did and he stood out accordingly.

Graham received a lecture position after graduation, but the position was fraught with problems. Graham couldn't keep his hands to himself and, as a result, one of the visiting professor's daughters got pregnant. Peter had, once again, been called into action to get his older brother out of trouble. With their father's money, a deal was made and Graham was off the hook. Just in the nick of time, an offer had come in for Graham to work at the atomic laboratory in Oak Ridge, Tennessee. His brother was included in the offer, but Peter had refused to go. A stern reproach from his father hadn't persuaded him, but the pleading look from his mother had. His father's open checkbook further convinced him. Peter mentally slapped himself for being so weak.

However, Peter made up his mind that this was the last posting he'd do for the infamous Dr. Graham Gresham. The guy was simply a magnet for trouble and his genius tended to be on the dark side. Graham was getting more unpredictable. He'd told Peter wild stories about conspiracy theories surrounding some of the work he did. Peter decided his brother was beginning to crack. The position in the United States might help Peter escape family pressures and, perhaps, Graham as well. The United States was a big country, and hopefully, one big enough that Peter could hide in.

Here he was, nearly two years later, not quite where he wanted to be, but making progress. Peter sighed, looking out the tiny office window. He hadn't escaped Graham, although he saw him less and less. Also, Peter had fallen in love with a young American secretary in another department named Jennifer. They had married, without his father and mother's permission, and had set up house just off the complex in the city of Oak Ridge. Jennifer was six months pregnant, staying home now to prepare for the baby's arrival.

Peter was as close to heaven as he felt he would ever get. Of course, that's usually when the roof caves in, which is what happened that morning Peter stared out the window.

His door abruptly pushed open. Peter looked over, surprised to see Graham for the first time in six months. He hadn't missed his brother at all.

"Peter! You've got to help me!"

THE TALL MAN with a frantic look on his face began pacing the small area of Peter's office.

"Take a load off, Graham. You're wearing out my linoleum."

Graham collapsed on a wooden chair by Peter's desk. "I'll never get used to American idioms. Just what does that mean 'take a load off'?"

Peter shook his head. "If you got your head out of your research lab and talked to a few Americans, you'd get it."

"It?"

"Yes, the idiom. What I meant by it."

Graham rolled dark eyes up to the ceiling. "You sound just like Father."

Peter's eyes flashed. "Blimey, I sure don't. Now what do you want? I need to get back to work."

Graham pointed a long, thin finger in his brother's direction.

"You aren't half as busy as me."

"Okay. You win the prize."

"What prize?"

"It's another American idiom, stupid."

He glared at Peter. "You and I both know that the last thing I am is stupid."

"You've acted stupidly in the past. Many times, actually."

"Acting stupidly and being stupid are two different things."

"So, this is why you interrupted my work today? To explain the difference in what it means to be stupid?"

"I haven't seen you in months. How's that darling wife of yours? Christie?"

"You don't even know my wife's name."

"Sure I do."

"It's not Christie."

"Sarah?"

"Not even close. It's Jennifer."

"I knew that. Mother is much aggrieved that you married an American."

Peter tried to tamp down his temper. "What do you want, Graham?"

Graham locked eyes with his brother. "I'm in trouble, Peter. Big trouble."

"You're always in big trouble."

"This time it's worse."

"No surprise there."

"You've got to help me."

"No, I don't. Call Father."

"Father would kill me."

"He would never kill the wonder child, the family star."

Graham's eyes widened with surprise. "Is that how you see me?"

"It's how I've always seen you, Graham. Now get out of my office. I have work to do." Peter turned toward his desk.

"I got a woman pregnant."

Peter didn't bother to turn back. "Again? Well, you're a big boy now and making a great salary. Do what you always do and pay them off."

"This one wanted more than I had. Lots more."

"So, call Father. He'll bail you out. He always has."

When Peter's comment met only silence, he turned back to his brother. Graham's face had reddened with beads of perspiration dripping down his face.

"What?"

"Her father is one of the Los Alamos scientists, a very big name."

"So?"

"She said he would have me deported if I didn't come up with the money. I can't go home now. I would be branded a disgrace."

"Is there an end to this story?"

"I didn't have enough to pay her off, Peter."

"Again, I ask, is there an end—"

"She asked me to send information to the Russians."

Peter's mouth dropped open. Completely speechless, he stared at his brother.

"Say that again."

Graham shook his head. "I don't dare."

"My office is secure."

"There are leaks everywhere."

"Apparently I'm looking at one."

Graham physically drooped. His eyes slid away. "Don't look at me like that, Peter. I couldn't get you to return my calls."

"I obviously didn't want to speak with you."

"Yes, well. I was left to muddle through on my own."

"And that's what you made of the situation: a muddle."

"It's much worse than that."

Peter scooted his chair closer to Graham. "This is serious stuff, Graham. How deep are you in?"

A weak smile appeared on Graham's face. "Another horrible American idiom."

"Tell me."

"This all started about five or six months ago."

"You've been...sending information," Peter glanced around his office before lowering his voice, "to the Russians?"

"Yes." Graham's word was pushed out with seemingly his last breath. His face paled and he gasped for air.

"Breathe, Graham."

"Peter, you've got to help me."

Peter's hands jerked up in defense. "Not this time. You've stepped over the line, and I can't help you. Turn yourself in."

"Are you nuts?" Graham's voice squeaked. "I can't do that."

"You could get a woman, what is she? Number three? You could get a woman pregnant and decide to betray your country, all without my help. You don't need my help to get out of it."

"Yes, I do."

"I repeat: turn yourself in."

"Father will kill me."

"Probably, but you deserve it this time." Peter shook his head. "You took advice from the wrong person —yourself."

"You wouldn't pick up the phone!"

"You are not blaming me for this mess!"

By this time, both brothers were perspiring. Graham looked worse, but Peter's collar had dampened.

"What should I do?"

"How long have you been meeting with Russians?"

"Five months, like I said. Maybe six."

"Five?"

"Maybe six. I tried to stop, but they won't let me. Now they're threatening to expose me here and in England. It would give Father a heart attack."

"And Mother. Plus, don't forget major jail time."

Graham hung his head.

"You've got to help me, Peter."

"What can I do? I'm a simple engineer with the brilliant scientist brother."

"You've got to think of something."

"Why me?"

"Because!"

"Because? That's a ten-year-old's answer."

"You've always helped me in the past."

Peter shook his head. "Not a good enough answer. I've always been forced to help by Father. He's not here. You're a grown man, Graham, and you can get out of your own messes."

Graham reached out to grab his brother's arm. "They threatened to kill me, Peter, and you."

"And *me*?"

"Yes, and your wife."

So, there it was. Once again, Peter Gresham was being forced to help out his older brother. This cycle had to stop.

"Peter, please. You're the only one I trust."

Peter sat immobile, not a breath stirring in the stuffy room.

"My life and my wife's life have been threatened by your foolishness?"

"Yes. These men mean business." Graham buried his head in his hands. "I'm so frightened, Peter. I'm so sorry to get you and your wife involved. Really I am."

Moisture leaked through his fingers. Peter blew out a weary breath and reached for a tissue to hand his brother.

"This is the last time, Graham."

Graham's head shot up. He dabbed at his watery eyes. "You'll help me?"

"Lord only knows how, but I'll have to think about it. How much time do you have?"

"I'm to make contact again tomorrow night."

"Well, that's not enough time to think of anything."

"Probably not."

Peter thought a minute. "Do what you have to do for now. I'll be in touch."

"Soon?"

"Yes."

Graham looked relieved, until panic slid over his face. "Oh, but don't tell Chris—Jennifer. Please."

"I have to, Graham! She's my wife and her life is on the line too."

"Oh, well, I guess so."

Peter's face twisted into a grim smile. "Did you know she's pregnant?"

"No!"

"Well, she's due in three months."

"Three months? Yes, so, um, congratulations."

"Your presence has just sucked all the happiness out of the room."

"I am so sorry, Peter, but you're the only one I can turn to."

Peter's mind raced with all the comments he wanted to throw in his brother's face. All the times he had to eat crow and do what their father asked. Looking at Graham, the hatred drained out onto the floor. This was life and death. It was time to put the bitterness behind him. If they could make it through this situation, the way ahead would be clear for Peter and his wife. The way would be different for his brother, but this had been coming on for a long time. Might as well get it over with.

That afternoon after much thinking, Peter Gresham walked into the office of Steven Simons, Head of Security for Oak Ridge National Laboratory. There was only one way out of this mess.

"Peter Gresham, is it?" The man behind the desk with thinning, gray hair stuck out his hand.

"Yes sir. Thanks for remembering my name."

"We met at the conference a few weeks back in Memphis."

"We did."

"Well, sit down, Peter. What can I do for you?"

Peter sat gingerly in a cushioned chair. It was too comfortable for what he was about to say. He moved around, trying to get prepared.

"Cat got your tongue, son?" Simons laughed at his little joke. "Come on. It can't be that bad."

Peter took a deep breath. "And what would you say if I told you it was worse than you can imagine?"

The smile faded on Steven Simons' face. After listening to what Peter had to say for a few minutes, he held up his hand.

"Stop there, Peter."

Simons picked up the phone.

ELEVEN

BLOOD

Phyllis sat at the tiny desk in the even tinier space she was given in the secretary pool. The enormous room held forty or so secretaries whose lives mainly consisted of taking dictation, typing letters and answering mail. All the women were about the same age, around twenty-five, and although they had the most mundane tasks to do, they acted like they had been given the blue ribbon at the state fair.

Apparently, their work gave them the satisfaction they needed and they bustled around energetically. Whenever a scientist or lab employee wandered into the pool, the women immediately straightened in their chairs and looked busy.

It was worse for Phyllis than working for George Martin in Washington because she didn't have Joe to go home to at night. She didn't have Lorraine to gossip with about Henry or office politics.

Pain gripped her. What Phyllis *did* have was a shooting pain on the left side of her body. She hadn't eaten much for breakfast and wondered if her body was letting her know she needed more food.

Putting aside her discomfort, she managed to stay on task with her letters until lunch. After a quick sandwich in the cafeteria, Phyllis headed for the restroom. A man bumped her when she came out, excused himself and hurried away. He was a tall, burly man, but she didn't see his face. Back at her desk in the secretarial pool, Phyllis reached into the pocket of her jacket for a tissue and her hand felt paper instead. Glancing around, she pulled out a small slip of paper with writing on it.

Meet me at Walgreen's on the corner after work. S sent me.

Her hand shook. S? That had to be Dick Simpson. Here was the contact she'd been expecting. Simpson was going to abort the mission. More than a year of waiting for an assignment and her first job was a disaster.

By the time she made her way to Walgreen's, her stomach tossed as if she were seasick. She felt warm and wondered why. The burly man who had bumped into her was sitting in a booth toward the back. He held up a hand. When she joined him, he waved to the seat across from him.

"Phyllis?"

"Yes."

"Mitch Ender. I work next to your husband."

Phyllis blinked wide eyes. "Joe sent you?"

He laughed. "No, ma'am. Major Simpson wanted me to make contact."

Just then a teenaged waitress popping bubble gum came up to their table.

"What would you like?"

"Coffee?" Mitch looked at Phyllis.

"Sure. That'll be fine."

"All you want is coffee?" Her bubble stayed out of her mouth before popping and slipping back in.

"For now, thanks."

She shrugged and left.

Phyllis and Mitch laughed at her frustrated departure.

"I don't think we made her day."

Phyllis' smile faded. "So, you've made contact. What did he say?"

Mitch glanced around the room, before lowering his voice. "We're to stay put awaiting further orders."

"Stay put?"

Mitch nodded. "He's trying to find out who leaked your mission. He's putting the mission on hold for a day or so."

"I thought he'd abort."

"Although I'm not in on all the particulars, my orders are to keep you safe and away from prying Russians." He raised a hand. "Does that make sense to you?"

"It does."

"Good."

The waitress walked over to deposit two cups on the table. Mitch and Phyllis watched as she determinedly poured coffee into the cups.

"Cream and sugar?"

"No, thanks. Phyllis?"

"Not for me either."

The young waitress shrugged again, not impressed with the customers at her table and stalked off.

"There's a fly in the ointment, Mitch."

"What's that?" Mitch took a sip of his coffee.

"The mission's already in play."

"How so?"

"I have a meeting scheduled tonight with the engineer." She shook her head. "I really can't go into all the details, if Major Simpson hasn't, so I won't. All I can say is that this meeting is paramount."

"I'll go with you. I'm to stay by your side."

"Where are you going to sleep?"

"Got a sofa?" Mitch gave her a crooked grin.

"You can come with me, but you can't speak. I can't jeopardize the mission."

"All right, but I'll have to phone it in."

She nodded. "That's fine."

TEN O'CLOCK FOUND Phyllis and Mitch sitting at a kitchen table in a nicely furnished apartment just off downtown Oak Ridge. Peter and Jennifer Gresham stared back at them.

"This is all happening too fast."

"What is, Peter?" asked Phyllis.

"It was barely a few weeks ago that I told Steven Simons about what Graham was doing."

"A few weeks can be a long time."

Peter fell silent. Jennifer threaded the fingers in her lap.

"Have you changed your mind?"

"No." Peter drew a deep breath. "I know what my brother has been doing is wrong. I want it to stop."

"But?" Phyllis prodded.

"I'm used to helping my brother. Turning him in and testifying against him is a big pill to swallow."

"You didn't cause Graham's problems."

Peter snorted. "Hardly, but I've always been the one to help him out of whatever trouble he was in. This is new territory for me."

"It's new territory for all of us."

The two couples fell silent. Water dripping from the faucet in the sink echoed through the room.

Phyllis tried again. "You made the first move to stop what your brother is doing. Do you wish now that you hadn't?"

"I wish my brother hadn't barged into my office and confessed his little secret."

"He needs to be stopped, Peter," added Phyllis.

"I know that. Don't you think I know that?" Peter exchanged a look with Jennifer. "He's betraying my country as well as yours."

"Yes."

Silence again overtook the room.

Jennifer cleared her throat. "May I speak?"

"Please do," said Phyllis.

"What I think my husband is trying to say is that his actions from here on out fly against everything he has ever done. It flies against everything his father taught him and everything he knows about family loyalty."

"What about loyalty to your country?"

She nodded, looked down in her lap. "That changes it all."

"Are you concerned for your safety?"

Peter looked startled. "Should I be?"

Phyllis stole a side glance at Mitch. "Your brother mentioned the Russians have threatened you and your wife. They aren't toying with your brother. If they learn you know anything, they won't play with you either. They'll want to keep him giving information, so you're a liability."

Peter's eyes blinked wide. "So, I'm in danger."

"And your wife."

"But—"

"Here's the deal as I see it, Peter and Jennifer," began Phyllis in a calm tone of voice. "Graham is giving the Russians much needed information about the atomic bomb. They're behind in nuclear technology and want to catch up as quickly as possible. Graham has been a success for them and they don't want him to stop."

"That's not surprising."

"We know much of what has been passed back and forth through other means."

"How do you know this?"

She shook her head. "I can't go into that. What I need to emphasize at this time is that you and your wife need to get out of here and to Washington as soon as humanly possible. That's the only way we'll be able to stop Graham."

"Jennifer's about to give birth."

"All the more reason for the rush." Phyllis felt a sharp twinge and laid a hand on her stomach. She winced uncontrollably.

Jennifer noticed her reaction. "Are you all right?"

"Yes, thank you." Phyllis looked at Peter. "Can we go over the plan?"

"Yes, ma'am." He glanced from Phyllis to Mitch. "You'll be assisting?"

"No, sir. I'm just the lookout."

Peter shrugged. "Okay, whatever. Let's get down to brass tacks, as you Americans say."

Phyllis smiled. "Yes, let's."

In Mitch's car on the way back to Phyllis' apartment, she and Mitch discussed the meeting.

"It went well, Phyllis?"

"Yes, very much. I think the mission is going to work."

"I'll need to let Simpson know. He may not like it."

"I'll proceed until he orders me to stop."

He pointed toward a phone booth by a street lamp.

"Let me call before we get back to your place."

"All right."

He pulled up in front of the booth and parked at the curb. While she watched him make the call, Phyllis felt something warm ooze in her underwear. Since Mitch was looking the other way, she pulled up her skirt to see what was happening. To her horror, bright red blood had stained her clothing and the passenger seat where she sat. She'd been too preoccupied to think about the pregnancy, but it was forefront in her mind now.

Phyllis rolled down her window.

"Mitch?"

He held up a finger and continued talking.

"Mitch?" she called a little louder.

Mitch covered the phone and leaned out of the booth.

"What?"

"I need to go to a hospital."

"Hospital?"

"And now, please."

With a puzzled look on his face, Mitch ended the call and ran back to the car.

"What's wrong?"

"I think I'm hemorrhaging."

He started the car and turned onto the street.

"Which way?"

"Two blocks and turn left."

Mitch looked over at her.

"Why would you be hemorrhaging?"

Phyllis carefully licked her lips. "I may be losing the baby."

"You're pregnant?" he fairly shouted.

"Joe didn't tell you?"

"Oh, for Pete's sake. No, he didn't." He shook his head. "That man can sure keep secrets."

Phyllis chuckled, then winced in pain. "You have no idea."

"Hang on, hon. We're almost there. I see it from here."

"Yes, good."

"You know, this is the second time this week I've taken a Schneider to a hospital."

He stopped the car by the emergency entrance, got out and walked around to help Phyllis.

"What did you mean by that?"

"Another time, dear Phyllis. Another time."

Mitch hurried Phyllis into emergency where an attendant rolled a wheelchair over to her. Mitch waved as she was taken into another room. He headed for the front desk to give the required information. Then he headed to a chair in the waiting room to worry and wait.

TWELVE

INVESTIGATION

A dark-haired woman with a grim look on her face sat in a metal chair by an old wooden desk. The brightly lit room held no interest for her. With bland walls and no decorations, the room's low ceiling made her feel claustrophobic and nervous. Her only desire was to get this over with.

The woman stared straight ahead unseeing, as the technician behind the desk pushed a few buttons on the strange-looking machine. The woman's hands lay on her knees and she squirmed at the tight bits of leather strapped to her chest.

"Ready?" asked the technician.

"Yes."

"Are you Maureen Sullivan?"

"Yes."

"Do you work for the Central Intelligence Agency as an analyst?"

"Yes."

"Were you divorced in 1943?"

"No."

"Do you live in Washington?"

"Yes."

"Have you ever leaked information about top secret missions to foreign entities?"

"No."

And on the questioning went for the next few hours on the fifth floor of the building that housed the CIA. Dick Simpson had wanted everyone on the floor tested by polygraph and so the process began. By noon, nearly everyone had been tested except for Simpson and his second in command, Captain Tom Metcalf. They both made appointments to be tested after lunch.

Later that afternoon, after everyone had been tested, Simpson and Metcalf pored over the findings of the polygraph. The few discrepancies they found were trivial in nature and not earth-shaking enough to be of use in discovering the source of the leak.

Simpson stared at the closed door of his office. He had hung a dartboard on it with a picture of Hitler in the middle. Metcalf stared at it with him.

"Maybe you should change it."

"Change what?"

"The picture."

"Picture?"

Tom pointed to the dartboard. "Your picture of Hitler. Maybe you should put up Stalin instead. Hitler is gone, remember?"

Dick's lips twitched into a smile.

"Actually, I was thinking about putting a picture of my ex-wife up there."

Tom laughed. "That might help us more than the polygraph."

Simpson turned to Metcalf. "What does that mean?"

"I just had a series of linear thoughts when you mentioned your ex-wife."

"Do you know her?"

"We've met at a few functions, but I can't say that I know her all that well."

"Well, what then?"

"What's her name?"

"Sandra."

"Well, here it goes. Sandra knows Suzy who knows Marian who knows Dorothy."

"You're not making any sense, Tom. What are you getting at?"

"Women have friends. Women talk to their friends."

Simpson was truly puzzled. "I don't follow you."

Tom moved his hand in a circular motion. "Women talk is my main point. Phyllis is a woman. Maybe she talked to someone."

"I get that, but I've known Phyllis a long time. She can keep things to herself."

"Sure, but who is that friend of hers? The one who's getting married soon?"

Simpson frowned. "That would be Lorraine, but she would never—"

"Lorraine works here too, right?"

"All the more reason for them to keep their mouths closed. There's a war on."

"Dick, there *was* a war on. Now it's clandestine. It's a cold war with spies, not a heated one with guns and bombs. Maybe Phyllis lowered her guard a little."

"And you think she might have blabbed to Lorraine,

who could have blabbed to someone else, and the word eventually got to a Russian agent?"

"Weirder things have happened."

Simpson stood abruptly, walked over to the dartboard. He ripped off the picture of Hitler, curled it into a ball and threw it into the wastebasket.

"I sure hope this doesn't go anywhere." He cast serious eyes at Metcalf. "Call in Lorraine."

THIRTEEN

LOSS

All she could focus on were the bright lights hanging overhead. The room smelled of antiseptic. An unsmiling woman with a white uniform bustled about, handing things to the doctor in charge. At least, Phyllis assumed he was a doctor. He was wearing a white coat with a stethoscope sticking out of a pocket. It was a good guess and something better to think about.

She was in a hospital and one of the worst things that could happen was happening to her. She was losing her baby.

What would Joe say?

Why was it happening?

Did she do something wrong?

Joe had been right—she should have passed up the assignment and stayed home.

"Mrs. Schneider?"

She should have stayed where it was warm and snug to protect the baby.

"Mrs. Schneider?"

Where it was safe and protected. Where it was—

"Mrs. Schneider!" A male voice punctured her thoughts. She blinked watery eyes at the man standing by her bed.

"Can you hear me?"

Phyllis swallowed. "Yes."

"I'm Doctor Talbert. Can we speak for a few moments? Then I'll let you sleep."

She pulled the thin blanket closer to her chin.

"Yes, all right."

"Are you aware of your circumstances?"

"Do I know I'm in a hospital? Of course."

"Do you realize you've had a miscarriage?"

Phyllis sighed, covered her chin with the blanket.

"Are you cold?"

"Very."

The doctor turned to the nurse. "Please get Mrs. Schneider another blanket."

When he turned back to Phyllis, she wet her lips.

"Yes, Doctor Talbert. I'm quite aware that I've had a miscarriage." Tears leaked from her eyes. "I know I lost my baby."

He handed her a tissue. "Miscarriages are common enough, but never easy to accept. I can have someone come in to talk with you, if you'd like."

Phyllis blotted her eyes, but the tears kept coming. "Perhaps I should."

"Everything is cleaned out now. You should be just fine."

"Just not pregnant anymore."

"No. I'm very sorry."

"Will I be able to get pregnant again?"

"Yes. As I said, miscarriages are very common, but

they don't generally stop a woman from getting pregnant again."

Silence filled the air while Phyllis considered what he said.

"Do you want me to ask your husband to step in?"

"My husband? He's here?"

"The man in the waiting room who brought you. I assumed he was your husband."

"No, doctor. He's just a friend."

"Do you want him to come in?"

She shook her head. "Not just yet. I'd rather speak with a professional first."

He smiled. "Certainly. I'll ask the therapist on the floor to visit you within the hour."

"When can I leave?"

"I'd like to keep you for a few more hours, just to be on the safe side. I want to make sure the hemorrhaging is quite over."

"Okay."

He turned to go.

"Oh, doctor?"

"Yes, Mrs. Schneider?"

"Could you get word to Mr. Ender in the waiting room that I will be a few more hours and ask him to wait for me?"

"I'll have it done."

"Thank you."

Once the nurse and doctor left, Phyllis pulled the blanket up over her head. What kind of failure was she as a woman and wife that she couldn't have a baby? Her body felt cold, almost foreign. How could it have turned on her like this? Hadn't she always tried to be a good person? A good wife? A good sister and daughter?

This was somehow her fault.

What did she do wrong?

The cold pervaded her whole body and she shivered uncontrollably. Two blankets weren't enough to warm her and she wondered if she would ever be warm again.

Sleep wouldn't come, despite the pill the nurse had given her.

Maybe sleep would never come again. Phyllis couldn't control the negative thoughts running through her mind like waves crashing a beach during a vicious storm. Just when she thought she couldn't stand it...

"Mrs. Schneider?" A woman's voice softly filled the air around her. Phyllis pulled the blanket down and opened her eyes.

"Yes. Who are you?"

"I'm Deidre Adams, one of the hospital's therapists. I was hoping we could talk for a few minutes. Are you up to it?"

Phyllis pushed up on the bed.

"Yes, I am."

"Good. Where would you like to begin?"

Phyllis sat up. She pushed the hair back from her face.

"I have a few questions."

FOURTEEN

JOE

Joe felt off all night. It wasn't the battle fatigue bothering him this time, it was a nagging thought that something was wrong.

He couldn't get ahold of Phyllis. The phone in her apartment rang and rang. He threw off the covers and struggled to his feet. When he'd paced the perimeter of the bedroom a few times, he yawned and headed to the kitchen. Lifting the lid off the coffee pot, the liquid smelled all right, but was cold as death. He plugged in the pot and patiently watched it begin to boil. Joe couldn't concentrate on anything at all, so watching the pot seemed like a good idea.

Work hadn't been going smoothly. He was working with several new recruits on logistics and weapons. If he didn't focus hard on the training topic, his mind would slip first to what had happened to him in Romania. Those thoughts were pushed aside as soon as he thought of them, but then an image of Phyllis would take their place. That wasn't helping his concentration either.

He would call a break now and then to collect himself and to be able to continue. But he was relieved when lunch came. The afternoon training was as bumpy as the morning, so he would give the recruits new assignments to work on and release them earlier than usual. They looked at him with questioning looks, but were happy enough to go work elsewhere on their homework. Joe dragged himself back to his cubicle on the third floor, and buried his gloomy thoughts with information for the next day's training.

He watched the coffee pot, willing it to finish its job.

Something was wrong. He felt it in his bones, even if he didn't know what it was. And it had to do with Phyllis, he was sure of it.

Finally, coffee perked noisily and Joe poured a strong cup with no sugar or milk. He knew it would keep him up the rest of the night, but he needed assurance and coffee fit the bill. He glanced out the window.

The first rays of sunshine burst through the kitchen window as the sun peeked over the horizon. Joe downed his cup of coffee, rose, and stretched before heading to the shower. He might as well get a jump on the day, since he was up anyway.

After a stirring shower and breakfast, Joe made his way to the office with his mind on today's lessons for the recruits. He'd have to keep a clear head, because it would take all he had to instruct on the gun range, not a place for mistakes. He caught the early bus and made his way to the third floor with no thoughts except for the gun lesson.

FIFTEEN

LORRAINE

Lorraine couldn't imagine why she was being summoned to the fifth floor. Since she didn't have the proper security clearance, a guard met her at the elevator and escorted her straight to Major Dick Simpson's office. Her anxiety kicked up a notch with every step she took. By the time they reached Simpson's office, she was a bundle of nerves.

"Lorraine! Please come in." Simpson's voice was friendly, but not enough to allay her fears. Goose bumps broke out on her arms and she wished she'd brought a sweater.

"Major Simpson." She stood stiffly by the door closed quietly behind her.

"This is Captain Metcalf. Have you met?"

Tom nodded to her.

"We have not, sir. How do you do, Captain Metcalf?"

"Fine, thank you. Pleasure to meet you."

"Please come in and take a seat," said Simpson.

Lorraine obliged with a weak smile. Nothing so far was helping her to relax.

"Thank you for joining us today, Lorraine. How is your work coming downstairs?" asked Simpson.

"Well, sir. You know that I work in the weather department."

"Oh, yes, of course." He glanced at Metcalf before proceeding.

"Now, Lorraine, I've asked you up here today to discuss a delicate matter."

"A delicate matter, sir? About what?"

"It's about...Phyllis Bowden, I mean Phyllis Schneider."

Her brows furrowed and she looked downright worried.

"Why did you ask me up here to talk about Phyllis? I thought you saw her more than I did."

Simpson smiled. "I doubt it, but I was wondering when you last spoke to her."

Lorraine bit her lip. "I haven't spoken to her since she left for Tennessee."

"Did she mention why she was going?" asked Metcalf.

Lorraine shook her head. "Not really. She said something about helping someone out, but she wasn't very clear." She glanced first at Metcalf and then at Simpson. "And I know enough not to ask questions."

"Why not?" asked Simpson.

"Sir, I work for the Central Intelligence Agency, remember? I know when to keep my mouth closed."

"Do you?" asked Metcalf.

Her eyes widened. "What do you mean by that?"

"Lorraine," began Simpson. "We know that you and Phyllis are close friends and have been for years."

"Of course you would know that, sir, since we both worked for you in London at the end of the war."

"Yes, of course, so you would know intimate details of her life."

"Possibly." Lorraine bit her lip again.

"Lorraine, do you know of something major happening in her life right now?"

"Major?"

"A big event. Maybe she didn't want to talk about it, but a few details slipped out anyway. You know, when you ladies are having a cup of coffee."

He could see Lorraine physically withdrawing. Her shoulders hunched and she scooted back in her chair. She knew something.

Lorraine's eyes darted around the room. Simpson could tell she was deciding what to say and what not to say.

"There is something big going on with her right now. She didn't want to tell me, but I was there when it happened. I pressed her for information and she finally told me what was going on."

Metcalf and Simpson traded a brief look.

"So, you know what she's been doing?" asked Metcalf.

"Yes. She finally told Joe too."

"She told her husband?" Simpson had a pained look on his face. "Why would she do that? Phyllis is a trained agent."

"Well, so is Joe, but this is different territory for both of them."

Metcalf looked confused. "How could it be different? Both of them have had tradecraft experience."

Lorraine laughed. "I don't think tradecraft experience is going to help either of them out in this case."

"Why not?" asked Simpson.

"You don't learn how to put on diapers, for starters," she replied with a smile. "And making baby formula isn't on the spy training agenda either."

Simpson's mouth dropped open. "What, in heaven's name, are you talking about?"

"Phyllis' big new event in her life."

"You mean the mission?"

"What mission?"

"The mission she's on."

Lorraine's lips parted as she sucked in a breath. "Phyllis is on a mission in Tennessee?"

Simpson shook his head. "Wait a minute. What are you talking about?"

"What are you talking about, sir?" Lorraine's head swiveled from Simpson to Metcalf and back. "I'm talking about her pregnancy."

Simpson leaped to his feet. "Her pregnancy?"

"She's pregnant?" asked Metcalf who had joined Simpson standing by the desk.

"Yes, sirs. I thought you knew."

"How would we know that?"

"Um, because she told you?" Lorraine chewed on a fingernail, eyes questioning. "You mean she didn't tell you and she's on a mission in Tennessee?" Her eyes shot up to the ceiling. "Oops, maybe I said too much."

Simpson's hands shot out in front of him. "No, Lorraine, you didn't over speak. I'm glad to know what's going on with her."

"I honestly thought you knew."

"We didn't."

"Okay. Now what? Will you bring her home?"

Simpson wearily plopped into his chair. Metcalf walked over to sit in his chair. Lorraine glanced from man to man. Simpson nodded to her and smiled.

"Thank you, Lorraine, for coming in today. We learned some valuable information."

"You're not going to tell her I told you, are you?" she asked. "Phyllis will get mad at me."

"No, it will be our little secret." He glanced at Col. Metcalf. "That's what we do here, isn't it? Keep secrets?" Metcalf smiled in response.

Simpson rose and extended his hand. "Thanks, Lorraine. You can go back to work now."

Lorraine stood to shake his hand. "Thank you, sir." She nodded to Metcalf. "Sir."

After she left, Simpson looked at Metcalf with disbelief in his eyes.

"Well, who could have guessed that, Tom?"

Metcalf shrugged.

"And you know what this means?"

"What?"

"We're back to square one in finding out who leaked the information about Phyllis' mission."

"Yep."

Just then there was a knock at the door.

"Come in," yelled Simpson.

Lorraine poked her head in. "Sir? I may have something for you."

"Come in. Close the door."

"As I was leaving, I had a thought. Maybe it's of no

value whatsoever, but then that's really up to you to decide."

"What's on your mind?" asked Simpson.

"Well...if there's one person in Washington, DC who knows everything about everyone, it's that old bookseller."

"What old bookseller?"

"Mr. Leto. He and Phyllis are good friends. She buys books there all the time."

"Why do you think he would be of interest to us?" asked Metcalf.

She grimaced. "I think he's fairly creepy, but Phyllis laughs when I say that. She thinks he's just a dodgy old man, but I think there's more to him than that."

"Mr. Leto? Where's the bookstore?"

"Down a couple of blocks by Walgreens downtown. You can't miss it."

"Thanks, Lorraine."

"Sir."

After Lorraine shut the door behind her, Simpson looked at Metcalf.

"Maybe we're not quite at square one after all."

"You don't think she's on to something, do you? Sounds crazy, Dick."

"I think she may be, Tom. It's certainly worth checking out." He rubbed his hands together. "Put a tail on this bookstore guy and have someone watch the shop. Let's get some data."

"Okay, Dick. I'm on it."

SIXTEEN

THE BOOKSELLER

Mr. Leto worked in his bookstore until late that night. New books had arrived and he needed to get them properly inventoried before he could stack them on shelves. It was hard work, as his stiff joints were reminding him. His back ached too. His assistant called in sick, so he was stuck with the whole job himself. If he had to bend over to pluck one more book from a box, he might not be able to straighten up.

After sniffling a few times, he took a crisp handkerchief from his pocket. His glance fell on a gnarled hand. It always surprised Mr. Leto that he was as old as he was. It seemed like only yesterday that he had a wife and children, but they were gone now. Gone with the past as if they never existed, or existed in another lifetime. His memories were yellow with age like an ancient book on one of his shelves. Dusty, yellow and beckoning for reconciliation.

He shook his head with disgust. Mr. Leto didn't want to remember the war—the first one or the second. He hadn't been able to help out as much with the second war as with the first, due to the onset of arthritis in his stiffening joints. And if he thought too hard, he would remember the bombing, the fire, and the screams that still haunted his dreams.

His hand knocked a book off his desk. Bending down to retrieve it, he read the title: *The Stranger* by Albert Camus. Memories fluttered like a cascade of butterflies. Leto had known Camus' father when they both lived in French Algiers. An image popped into his mind about young Camus reading a book under a tree. Such a serious youngster who grew up to be a rebel. Resistance and rebelliousness—watchwords for Camus. He and Camus crossed paths a few times during the war when they both lived in Paris. With Camus' published writings, Leto knew of Camus' flirting with Communism. But the Russians were allies then, and it didn't seem to matter. How complicated the various philosophies became during and after the second war. How mixed became patriots, or those who fancied themselves to be so.

Those thoughts must have been in Mr. Leto's mind when he wrote the note and slipped it into another copy of *The Stranger*. He'd already been pressured to get involved since Phyllis Bowden visited his shop frequently. But after developing a friendly and fatherly relationship with the young woman, Leto had changed his mind. Thus, the warning note. She needed to know the Cold War could heat up fast and she should get out while she could. Staring at the book, he confused her image with his daughter and that, he thought grimly, was reason enough for his action. Screw Igor and the rest.

As he wandered past his desk and through the store,

his leg hurt more than usual. He'd broken it in so many pieces after the fire that the doctor said it would never heal properly. The doctor was right. Not an hour went by that Leto was not reminded of that rescue he attempted so long ago. Of how he nearly perished trying to save those now lost to him. Many times, he wished he had perished with them.

But Phyllis. Saving her might be all he could do in the time he had left. That was all right. He'd lived a good, long life and had accomplished more in his life-time than most people. He was content to face what-ever repercussions might be coming his way. If Igor found out, he wouldn't be pleased. That was all right too. Once comrades during the war, the Cold War had made them quasi-enemies with different agendas. Igor wanted to keep fighting, while Leto just wanted to be left alone.

As he tidied up to leave, hairs on the back of his neck prickled. It was a reaction from war days that put him on guard.

He was being watched.

Senses alert, he looked around his store with new eyes, eyes searching every detail of the shop he knew by heart. There was something new here, something unwanted. He knew from past experience that someone in the dark was watching him.

The Russians?

The Americans?

Perhaps he shouldn't have sent that note to Phyllis. Perhaps he should have minded his own business and stayed invisible as he had managed to do for so many years.

He turned back toward his desk. A sudden motion

made him twist his head to see what was behind him. That's when he felt pain on the top of his head before the world blacked out.

"SIR. THAT'S MY REPORT."

"You've hardly said anything in it." Dick Simpson stared at the paper in front of him. "He goes to the store, he goes home. He goes to the store, he goes home." He looked up at the agent. "That's it? That's all that ever happens to this guy?"

"We've put taps on his phone and have watched the store. He lives upstairs, but nothing happens out of the ordinary. He rarely goes out." The agent shifted position. He knew his report wasn't being accepted well. "What else do you want me to do?"

"No one goes in there who might be slightly suspicious?"

"No sir. We've tracked the customers we saw and they're all legitimate."

"Really?"

"Yes, sir."

Simpson looked up at the agent with a sour expression on his face. "Bring him in. We need to talk to him."

"Yes, sir."

After the agent left, Simpson loosened his tie. He glanced at the dartboard on the back of his door. He'd removed the picture of Hitler, but a new picture was needed.

"Damn. I need to get a break here."

An hour later, Simpson received a call from the agent watching Mr. Leto's bookstore.

"Major Simpson?"

"Yes."

"Sir, there's been a development at the bookstore. I think you should come here."

"You want me to come to the bookstore?"

"Yes, sir. Now would be a good time."

Simpson paused. "On my way."

SEVENTEEN

MAJOR SIMPSON

When Major Dick Simpson parked his car, lights blazed from the little bookstore. A pretty little corner shop, he mused, that probably did much foot traffic on the busy downtown Washington street. A sign in the window announced that he bought books as well as sold them. Looking through the front window, Simpson could see books stacked on bookshelves as high as the ceiling. The man certainly had a huge inventory.

Walking in, Simpson's nose immediately smelled the dust associated with books, but walking in further, he smelled something else. Something sweet, yet unpleasantly so. The smell of blood.

"Agent Stiles? Are you back here?"

"Come around here, sir," called the agent. "He was found by the register."

Simpson looked down on the floor at the man laid out before him. An elderly man with grizzled, white hair. His head had been bashed in and was currently residing in a pool of blood. One pocket of the blood-stained pants revealed a white handkerchief poking out.

Watery eyes, dead to the world, stared straight ahead. Glasses stuck out of a shirt pocket. Books lay scattered all around.

"Mr. Leto?" asked Simpson.

"Yes, sir."

"You've made the necessary calls?"

"Yes, sir. Local police and ambulance in route."

"Unnecessarily so," muttered Simpson as he bent down to examine Mr. Leto more closely.

"Sir?"

Major Simpson shook his head. He was too late to find out what this man knew, but he had a gut feeling that he had known too much. Someone obviously thought so, unless this was just a random robbery.

"Anything missing from the register?"

The agent shook his head. "Don't think so. The drawer is shut tight and there's no evidence of tampering."

"And we wouldn't know if there was anything else missing." Simpson took in Leto's clothes and position of death. Something caught his eye. "What's this?"

Smudges written in blood lay on the floor next to the body down around one hand. Simpson pointed them out to the agent. "What does that look like to you?"

Stiles squinted at the floor. "It could be an 'i' there, sir."

"Yes. Yes, it very well could be." Simpson straightened and brushed off his slacks. "We might have a message here, Agent Stiles."

"Yes, indeed, sir, but what is it?"

Simpson didn't respond to Stiles. At that moment, emergency personnel came through the door, tools of their trade in hand. A local police officer and serious-looking man dressed in a neat suit and topcoat walked ahead of a photographer. Simpson guessed the man in the dark suit was a DC detective.

"Make sure I get a copy of the photos, Stiles."

"Yes, sir."

Knowing a dead end when he saw one, Major Simpson took a last look around the shop. The hard look told him no more than when he had walked in, lights blazing from the corner bookstore. The little bookstore where a chapter of Phyllis' life had come to a deadly close. Simpson needed to know more about Leto and he needed to know now.

As the detective took in the scene, he walked briskly toward Simpson with a no-nonsense expression quickly becoming a frown.

"Who are you?"

"CIA."

"And how would I know that? Got a badge?"

Dick smiled. "I guess you're just going to have to trust me."

The detective snorted. "That would be a first." A long hard look at the body had the man taking out a small notebook and pen. He jotted down a few details until Simpson interrupted.

"Excuse me, Detective?"

"Carrothers."

"Detective Carrothers?"

Carrothers glanced over at Dick Simpson. They contrasted sharply. Carrothers wore a wool suit with a winter overcoat and black fedora. Simpson wore an Army uniform with questioning eyes that Carrothers could read.

"I realize this isn't our jurisdiction."

"So why are you here?"

"I can't tell you. It's a case of national security."

"Of course."

"But I can tell you this."

Carrothers put his pen in a pocket. "I'm listening."

"Whatever I can find out about the dead man, the better."

"Better for who?"

Simpson shook his head.

"It's a state secret. I'm sorry."

Carrothers put away his notebook to crouch next to Leto, lying on the floor. He examined every inch of the scene before speaking.

"I've dealt with your type before."

"What type is that?"

"The type that won't talk to cops." He straightened to look Dick in the eye. "You spy types think you're more important than us locals and that's definitely not the case."

The situation was beginning to sour. Simpson had to think of something. Quick.

"Look. This is your investigation. I'm not butting in."

"And yet you're still here."

"Because I've got a favor to ask."

"I don't do favors."

"You do this one favor for me, and I'll see if I can help you somewhere down the line."

"You giving me a marker?" asked the detective with narrowing eyes. "I ain't no gumshoe. You better be legit."

Simpson tried to hold back his eyes from rolling

upward. He crossed his chest and stuck three fingers in the air.

"You're no boy scout either, Detective, and I'm sure we could help one another in the future. It's good to have a few connections."

Detective Carrothers spent the next few moments checking out the shine on his black shoes. He rubbed one against his pant leg before looking back at Simpson.

"What do you want, Mr. CIA?"

"A look around upstairs."

"What's upstairs?"

"This man's apartment. He's a possible key to something big happening right now."

"Big?"

Simpson nodded. "Massively big, but that's all I can say."

Carrothers' lips puckered in thought. He seemed to come to a decision. He reached for a card inside his jacket pocket and handed it over to Dick.

"Here's my card. If I should ever call over to the CIA, I expect you to get back to me. That's my condition."

"Done." When Detective Carrothers didn't look like he believed him, Simpson tried again. "I'm a man of my word."

Carrothers flicked a look upstairs.

"Five minutes and don't touch anything."

"Got it. Thanks, Detective."

"My pleasure." Carrothers turned back to the photographer to issue a few instructions. Dick took that as his sign to move. He signaled to the agent waiting just out of earshot.

"Agent Stiles?"

"Yes, sir?"

"You say he lived upstairs?"

"That's right."

Simpson lowered his voice. "Have you been up there before I arrived?"

"Not yet. I was waiting for you."

Simpson nodded. "Let's take a look."

"This way, sir." Agent Stiles led him to a staircase toward the back.

The creaky staircase needed to have a few boards nailed back down. Other than that and a fresh coat of paint, Dick thought the staircase leading to the apartment above the bookstore was in decent shape, despite its age. The old brick building that housed the bookstore had been built many years ago. He half expected the apartment to look like a shabbily constructed storage closet.

So, when he opened the front door—handy that Agent Stiles just happened to have a key—Simpson was moderately surprised. He had visited homes of elderly people and found the premises to be generally musty, outdated and usually messy. For some reason, older folks collected every newspaper and magazine that came to their door.

Not so with Emile Leto's apartment.

The neatly arranged living room caught Dick's eye first. The furniture was old, to be sure, but it had been taken care of properly and was still very usable.

A sofa against one wall had the telltale signs of age with worn threading, but a blue and red plaid throw covered the bulk of it with style. A coffee table of dark wood faced the sofa and a chintz chair with a beige cover completed the conversation area. With a deep recess in the cushion, Dick guessed it was Leto's favorite chair. Two French magazines sat on the coffee table, waiting patiently to be read. French? Of course. Emile Leto was from French Algiers. Apparently, he kept up with events in France. Seemed reasonable.

A small dining room to the left held a table and chairs of a similarly dark wood; Dick guessed mahogany, although he realized he was inexperienced with furniture wood identification and left it at that. With little dust on the various furniture pieces, Dick surmised Leto must have taken care with his property.

Two windows in the living area looked out over the street below. Simpson glanced out to see Detective Carrothers talking to another police officer in a patrol car parked at the curb. Carrothers looked up to catch Simpson in the window. Although Dick smiled, the detective didn't return his greeting.

Window covers had been pulled up for the day to let the sun into the apartment. The windows weren't as dirty as Simpson expected them to be, and he appreciated the small plant sitting in the window on the sill. It had recently been watered.

A collection of postcards were framed and hung on a wall. Peering closely, Simpson could make out scenes of life in a few French towns. An ancient post office was on one card with a quaint café on another. He noted the cards were from decades past, showing a life that was no more.

Dick checked out the floral carpet as he made his way to the bedrooms. Not the kind of flooring he preferred. Something quiet to settle him after a hard day was his preference. Maybe Leto had been married at one time and this is what his wife had wanted. The size and abundance of red roses in the thinning carpet could give him a mild headache, so Simpson quickened his pace.

Again, he was surprised. There were three fairly good-sized bedrooms in the upstairs apartment. Mr. Leto must have had some decent money when he came to town to be able to afford to buy the store and accompanying apartment. Even if he had bought the place twenty years ago, the price was still too high for Agent Stiles' budget today. Simpson nodded to his agent.

"We need to find out where Leto got his money for this place."

"Yes, sir."

Dick walked into the master bedroom. Larger than the other two, a double bed sat in the middle of the room with a small table and lamp next to it. Two dressers, one large and one small, graced the walls with a small mirror above the large dresser. The furniture resembled something his grandfather would have liked, although the effect was cozy and looked lived in. Picture frames dotted the dressers with smiling people. Stiles took pictures of everything as he followed behind Simpson.

"We need to identify the people in these photos."

"Yes, sir."

Simpson cocked an ear toward the hallway. Hearing nothing, he removed a hanky from his pocket. Shaking his head at Stiles, Dick used the hanky to open a dresser drawer. The first one stopped him cold.

"Look here."

Agent Stiles peered into the drawer over Simpson's shoulder. "Looks like a ring."

Simpson's cloth-draped fingers picked up the ring to

hold it higher. "I need a better look." The shiny silver ring with a curious engraving reminded him of something Phyllis had told him about the Russian agent she met on the train to Tennessee. Didn't she mention a ring he was wearing? He'd have to check his notes.

"Get a picture, Stiles."

Dick's mind was working overtime as he carefully replaced the ring back to the tray where he'd found it. Just as carefully, he closed the drawer and quickly checked the others. Having what he needed, Dick straightened to tuck the handkerchief back in his pocket.

"Done, sir?"

"I believe so. Let's get out of here, Agent Stiles. I do believe I hear Detective Carrothers' heavy footsteps on the staircase. Our time has come to a close."

Carrothers entered the apartment as Simpson and Stiles were leaving the bedroom.

"Get what you wanted?"

"I did, thanks."

The detective and his uniformed officer watched the men leave the apartment. When the door closed behind them, Dick nodded.

"And that, as they say, is that."

He had work to do and it was time to get back to the office.

WHEN SIMPSON GOT BACK to his office, Col. Metcalf met him at the door with papers in hand.

"Got a minute, Dick?"

"Sure. Come on in."

"Where were you?"

"Close the door."

After the door closed, Simpson crossed to his desk.

"Sit down, Tom. Listen, I just got back from visiting that bookstore Lorraine told us about. Remember?"

"Yes, the old bookseller, Mr. Leto."

"I had him checked out and the agent doing the stake-out called me this morning."

"What's up?"

"Leto was murdered."

"Murdered? When?"

"Not sure. I didn't wait for the coroner. I don't have the time."

"But murder? You're sure?"

Simpson nodded. "And by someone who knew how. But still..."

"Still what?"

"He was able to write a letter in blood before he succumbed."

"Oh, come on, Dick. You're not falling for that, are you?"

Simpson's eyes widened. "What do you mean?"

"It's the oldest trick in the book to steer authorities away from the real killer. What was the letter?"

"It looked like an i."

"I? As in innocent?"

"Right."

Metcalf locked eyes with Simpson. "Maybe the infamous Igor who met Phyllis on the train?"

"That's what I'm thinking."

"Too obvious."

"Why? We're the only ones who know about him, besides Phyllis, of course." Simpson glanced down at the cup on his desk. He picked it up and traced the rim. "And I found a ring in the upstairs apartment, Tom."

"What kind of ring?"

"A silver ring with engraving that sounds similar to what the Russian was wearing when Phyllis met him."

"What's the tie-in?"

"I'm guessing that Leto knew Igor. It might be a stretch, but the Allies were friends with the Russians during the war. Maybe the men knew each other."

Tom rubbed his chin. "Maybe they worked together in the French resistance. That isn't really a stretch; it's believable."

"I think so too. Interesting too that the Russian was still wearing his and Leto's was in a drawer."

"But he hadn't thrown it away."

"No. The rings were significant to both men."

Tom paced the length of the room twice before glancing back at Simpson.

"So, if Leto knew Igor, that doesn't look good for Leto. He must have been a spy or mole we didn't know about." Metcalf shrugged. "Doesn't look good for us either. We should have had that information. For Pete's sake, Leto has been in that bookstore for years probably."

"There could be all kinds of moles around the city that we aren't aware of. Nature of the game."

Simpson laced his long fingers and set them on his desk. He twirled his thumbs idly. Both men watched his fingers dance as minutes ticked by.

"Listen. While you were out, I did some background research on Leto."

Simpson stared at Metcalf. "Let's hear it."

Tom took off his jacket to settle in a chair. He

picked up several papers sitting on Simpson's desk and began reading.

"Emile Albert Leto was born 1877 in French Algiers to working class parents. His father was a businessman who had fought in the Crimean War. Leto studied architecture at the University of Algiers, getting a degree in 1902."

"So, he was an architect?"

"Apparently."

"Phyllis had guessed that. Where did he work?"

"He set up a business in Paris after graduation and was successful for several years. He married a Parisian woman and had one daughter."

"Any war involvement?"

"Yes, he was in the French resistance in World War I. No record of any involvement in WWII."

"So, he could have known the Russian in 1914 or thereabouts."

Tom nodded. "Could have happened. France and Russia were allies in foreign policy and strategic military interests. Igor Ivanov could have worked with the French resistance and met Emile Leto."

"Anything further?"

"We're still checking."

"Okay. Let me know when you have more."

Silence overtook the men as Metcalf picked up another sheaf of papers off Simpson's desk. Dick stared thoughtfully at the dartboard on the back of his door.

"I've been thinking."

Tom looked up. "Yeah?"

"I'm thinking that Leto could have been the leak."

"How'd you get that idea?"

"I've been tossing over ideas on how it happened. I need more data for a conclusion."

"Well, I've got an idea of my own."

Simpson looked over at the neatly dressed officer. Every detail of his uniform was straight and polished. Metcalf could have stepped off a recruiting poster.

"Tell me what you've got."

Metcalf offered the papers in his hand. "Take a look."

Simpson accepted the papers, scanned the first page and then the second. "Is this what I think it is?"

Tom smiled. "It could be. This information was just turned in to me. Agent Meriweather flunked the polygraph."

"He flunked?"

"There were...shall we say, discrepancies. Enough for us to call him on the carpet. Maybe Meriweather knew Leto."

Simpson placed the papers in a neat pile, before straightening his tie. "One way to find out." He pressed the call button on his intercom. "Sarah?"

"Yes, Major Simpson?"

"Call in Ed Meriweather, please."

Ed Meriweather walked into Major Simpson's office slowly, each step slower than the first. His dark suit hung off his hulky build like a sheet wrapped around a rock. With black wavy hair, a strong chin and attractive features, Simpson wondered why he wasn't modeling for a men's magazine, instead of working as an analyst at the Central Intelligence Agency. His guilty look didn't cast him as an innocent person.

"Meriweather?" asked Simpson from behind his desk. He didn't extend his hand in greeting.

"Yes, sir."

"I don't believe we've met. Where precisely do you work?"

"I analyze reports for overseas personnel, sir."

Simpson nodded to the chair in front. "Please have a seat."

"Thank you." Meriweather sat stiffly with his back ironing board straight. He clasped nervous hands in his lap.

"Relax, Meriweather," said Col. Metcalf. "This isn't an inquisition."

"Yes, sir." Meriweather leaned back into the chair, but looked no more relaxed than when he shuffled in.

Simpson glanced at the papers on his desk. He ran a finger along one line and looked up at Ed Meriweather.

"I'll be blunt. You flunked the polygraph."

Ed's eyes blinked wide. "Flunked? How did I do that?"

"Apparently by not telling the truth," replied Simpson. He held up the first paper with wavy lines that dipped. "See this?"

Ed squinted to see the paper. "Not without my glasses, sir."

"So put them on."

Ed pulled a pair of glasses from his coat pocket and set them neatly on his face. When he peered at the paper in front of him, he bit his lip.

"See this line?" Dick pointed at the paper. "And this one? Every time you were asked a question about your personal life, it was determined from your responses that you were not telling the truth."

Meriweather's left eye twitched, but he said nothing.

"Do you have anything you want to tell us, Meriweather?" asked Col. Metcalf. "Now's the time to get whatever it is off your chest. If we find out independently, it could be worse for you."

Ed Meriweather's face puckered like he'd bit into a lemon. He didn't appear to be breathing and his cheeks puffed like he was about to explode.

"Meriweather?" prompted Simpson. "Out with it."

"I didn't know, sir." Words burst out of Meriweather like an exploding dam.

"Didn't know what?" asked Simpson.

"I didn't know who she was."

"Who's she?"

Meriweather took off his glasses and bent his head. He whispered a name so softly that both Simpson and Metcalf leaned forward.

"What? Speak up."

Meriweather raised his head and looked directly at Dick. "Your wife, sir. Sandra Simpson."

Simpson looked like he'd been smacked across the face.

"My ex-wife, you mean."

"She said her name was Sandra O'Connor. We met at one of the agency functions last year."

Simpson glanced over at Metcalf whose eyebrows were deeply furrowed in confusion. "That was her maiden name."

"You were seeing my wife?" Dick asked Meriweather.

"Yes, sir."

"When did this start?"

Meriweather swallowed hard before answering. "Around Christmas last year, sir."

Metcalf spoke to Simpson. "You were still married then." Simpson held up a hand.

"You say you didn't know she was my wife?"

"No, sir." Ed's lower lip quivered. "Please don't fire me, sir. I didn't know."

"That's what you were thinking about when you answered some of the polygraph questions?"

Ed nodded. "I thought you were on the rampage because I know you got divorced. I didn't know who your wife was until I saw a picture of her on your desk last summer."

"Last summer? You were seeing her last summer?"

"Yes, sir."

Simpson sat back in his chair. "Are you still seeing her?"

"No, sir."

"Well, that's for the best, Meriweather. She wasn't one for sticking to the truth."

"I guess not, sir."

Meriweather's back straightened again. "Am I fired, sir?"

Simpson laughed, shook his head. "No, but I want to thank you."

"For what?"

Simpson waved his hand. "Get back to work, Ed, and don't think any more about this conversation. The subject is dead and buried, all right?"

"Yes, sir."

After Ed Meriweather left the office more quickly than when he had entered, Simpson smiled at Metcalf.

"What are you grinning about, Dick?"

"Sandra sold me a bill of goods about why she wanted a divorce. She blamed me for our lack of children and the various postings around the world and a myriad of other things. According to her, I was a first-rate heel and scumbag. Didn't understand her and all that crap." He laughed. "Turns out she just wanted to play the field."

"Guess she was cheating on you with Meriweather," said Tom. He stifled a smile. "How do you feel about that?"

"You sound like a damn psychiatrist, but I won't hold that against you."

"Thanks, I think."

Dick's serious eyes stared straight toward the door. "I'm glad to finally know the truth. You know that expression? The truth will set you free?"

Metcalf nodded.

"That's exactly how I feel: relieved and free. I thought I'd done everything wrong in that marriage. It wasn't me, but her wanting out is all." He turned toward Tom. "I can't tell you how much better I feel."

"Good enough to start dating again?" Tom smirked and rose from his chair.

"Very funny. Maybe, maybe not, but I feel a weight off my shoulders."

Metcalf started for the door.

"Where are you going?"

"To work. We've gossiped enough about your sex life."

Both men laughed. Simpson glanced at his watch. "You're right. It's time to get back to work. Find out what the research says about Leto, will you? I'm going to try to track down Phyllis. I haven't heard from her or Ender for a while and it's making me nervous."

"Sure thing, Dick."

EIGHTEEN

PETER

"Tonight's the night, Jennifer." Peter Graham stood at the kitchen sink looking out a window into the dark, empty street in front of his house. He glanced back at his wife. Her pretty blonde hair curled around her face made her look younger than she was. But her eyes were dark with worry and she rubbed her stomach with nervous fingers.

"What's wrong? Are you having contractions?"

Jennifer shook her head. "No, but the baby has been moving a lot lately. He's probably as nervous as I am."

"I know how he feels. I know how *you* feel." Peter ran a hand through his messy hair. Jennifer stepped close enough to grab his hand, kiss it and then smooth his hair for him. "Thanks, sweetie." He bent forward to lightly kiss her lips. "I know you're scared. We both are."

"So, what are we going to do, Peter?" She looked at the clock on the kitchen wall. "We're set to meet Phyllis in two hours."

Just then the phone rang. In the stillness, Peter jumped at the sound, grabbed at it hanging on the wall.

"Yes. Hello."

"Peter?"

Peter sagged with relief. "Graham?"

"Who did you think would be calling?"

"What do you want?"

"I'm thinking about not going tonight."

"To meet up with—"

"Don't say it over the phone, Peter."

"Right. Okay, then what are you going to do?"

Peter knew the feds were already watching his brother, but he couldn't let on about that or what was about to happen.

"I'm not sure. What do you think I should do?"

"Graham, I told you it would take time to think through this mess and come up with an answer for you."

"Yes, well, I'm scared. These guys play for keeps." Graham lowered his voice and spoke menacingly. "And you know you're in this thicket with me, remember? They've threatened to harm you and your wife."

Peter rolled his eyes. "Enough with the George Raft dialogue. You been watching old movies on the telly again?"

"What in the King's name are you talking about?'

"Never mind. Just do what you want, Graham. You always have."

"But whatever I do has implications for you."

"Don't I know it," Peter muttered to himself.

"What?"

"I don't have any answers for you. Do what you think you should do."

"I probably should meet them." Graham sighed. "They'll just hound me until I do."

"Great life you've carved out for yourself, brother."

"Well, I never thought anything like this would happen when I was dating some girl."

"She wasn't just some girl, Graham." Peter's words burst out in a huff. "And you weren't being careful sexually either."

"Okay, okay. You've made your point." Silence filled the line for a tense moment. "I'm going to go. I'll call you later."

"I won't be here, Graham."

"Where will you be?"

Peter glanced at Jennifer. Her wary eyes questioned him.

"We'll be out visiting friends. Call me tomorrow."

"All right. Later then."

"Good-bye, Graham."

Peter replaced the phone in the cradle carefully. His lips stretched into a tight grin.

"What? What are you thinking, Peter? You have that crafty look on your face again."

Peter laughed, took ahold of Jennifer's hand. "When have you ever seen a crafty look on my face?"

"Never mind. Tell me what's going on."

"Get packed, honey. We're getting the hell out of here."

"To meet Phyllis?"

"Oh, no. We're in way over our heads and I'm booking the first flight anywhere."

"Peter..."

"I know, I know. We run and our problems run with

us, but we've got a baby to think of, honey. It's not just about us."

"You're having second thoughts about turning in your brother."

Peter nodded. "Second, third and fourth thoughts. It's all too scary for words. Let's just go, figure something out later from a distance."

"Maybe you should have thought of that before you went to see the Director of Security."

"Yeah, maybe. In the meantime..."

"We pack."

Leaving the cozy kitchen, Peter grabbed two suitcases from the hall closet. "Just necessities. We can buy other things when we get where we're going."

If we make it that far. The thought ran through Jennifer's head that they were making a grim mistake, but she was too caught up in protecting her baby. She packed a bag.

NINETEEN

THE MISSION

"Are you sure you're up to this, Phyllis? You don't look so good."

"Thanks for the vote of confidence, Mitch. You're a real cheerleader."

Mitch shivered and stamped his feet. "It's cold out here and you need more than a cheerleader. You need your head examined."

She scanned the area by the apartment building before coming back to Mitch. "Have you heard anything further from Major Simpson?"

"No, but—"

"Has he said to abort the mission?"

"No."

"So, we carry on as planned."

"Phyllis." Mitch Ender tugged her coat more tightly around her and adjusted her scarf. "You just got out of the hospital."

Phyllis pushed his hand away. "I realize that."

"And you lost your baby."

"I'm an agent first."

"No, you're a woman first and you can't ignore what just happened."

She pulled on her gloves. "I'm not ignoring anything. I'll deal with the miscarriage after the mission."

Mitch shook his head. "This isn't going to end well. I feel it in my bones."

"You and your bones can take a hike, Mitch. I've got this covered."

"Phyllis..."

"Would you mind getting those other gloves from the car for me? These aren't very warm and we have to stay here for a while longer until Peter and Jennifer show up." She gave him her warmest, most innocent smile.

"All right. Stay put. I'll be right back."

Phyllis stared at the scene. Her eyes blinked fast, and her thoughts came faster. The decrepit apartment building where she was to meet with her targets was too dark, too quiet. Too empty. Something felt off.

The snow-covered street showed no footsteps. Cars parked on both sides were close together allowing no room for mistake. They looked as boxed in as Phyllis felt. Stifled by Mitch, ignored by Simpson, now she was as barren as the unoccupied streets. Pushing an image of a dark-haired chubby baby from her mind, she glanced at Mitch's retreating back before slipping around the corner of the building. No streetlights here to illuminate her escape. Joe had always told her to rely on her instincts and her training approved the idea. She felt that something was wrong.

Walking briskly along buildings that would give no welcome, she felt the sound before it registered. Footsteps behind her. Wanting to meet no one, she quickened her pace. Senses alert, she felt for the gun in her pocket, put chilly fingers around the handle for confidence. The footsteps wouldn't be Mitch. He wouldn't have had time to grab the other pair of gloves and catch up with her this fast. Someone else was on her tail, someone unwanted. She knew it.

Slipping around another corner, she glanced back to identify the stalker. A dark figure wearing a long, black jacket. The face was obscured with little lighting and lowered hat. The figure turned the corner too, not bothering to pretend he was doing anything other than following her.

Meant to scare? Meant to frighten her off?

Hurrying now down another block with more cars parked closely to the curb. It was hard footing with the slick snow, but she couldn't slow down. Another set of footsteps joined the first. Some place to hide became a top priority. Peter and Jennifer hadn't shown and something had gone wrong with her plan.

Phyllis felt a trickle of liquid down one leg. Oh, no. It couldn't be. An alley was coming up on her right. She turned sharply and noticed a dumpster parked by the side. Few lights illuminated her way causing the darkness all around to appear more sinister. Ignoring seeds of panic, Phyllis climbed into the dumpster. Her nose wrinkled when accosted by a myriad of repugnant smells: stale food, burned paper, crushed boxes, unidentifiable aromas making her stomach queasy. She fought a sudden desire to retch.

Phyllis squatted low, pulling part of a cardboard box around her. The collection of food smells reminded her that she hadn't eaten in quite a while. Deep breaths calmed her somewhat and she could concentrate on outside sounds. Darkness crept around her like a blanket. But instead of comfort, she felt fingers of doubt poke at her confidence. The blackness of the night reflected how she felt at losing the baby, maybe losing her job.

In the dead of night with the cold weighing her down, Phyllis pulled out her weapon automatically. Squatting low with her gun poised toward the lip of the dumpster, Phyllis knew she could wait it out. In a way, darkness was her friend and she was thankful for the clouds covering the stars. With little light, she felt as safe as she could be.

In the heat of the moment, nothing occupied her mind but the mission. And when she heard a noise outside the dumpster, steady hands gripped the gun. Adrenaline pounded a steady beat in her ears. A head came into view. She cocked the pistol.

"Hold it, Phyllis! Don't shoot me!"

She exhaled shakily. "Mitch?"

"Yeah, it's me, hon. Put down the gun."

She lowered her weapon before pushing her way out of the cardboard box. Standing, her legs shook with cold and nerves.

"I was followed."

"I know. Come on. Let's get you out of there."

Lifting her hand to him, Mitch tugged her upright. "What the hell were you doing hiding in a dumpster?"

"I told you—I was being followed."

"And so, you eluded them by climbing into this smelly thing. Ick."

After he'd helped her out of the dumpster, Phyllis managed a small smile. "Thanks."

"You're welcome."

"How'd you find me?"

"I followed your stalker after you ditched me. He led me here, but took off when he caught on that I was tailing him."

"Russians?"

"Probably." Mitch took her hand. "You're freezing. Come on. Let's get you cleaned up. Apparently, the mission didn't go off tonight."

"No. Something happened to Peter and Jennifer."

"Cold feet maybe."

"Maybe. I hope nothing worse than that."

"Yeah. Let's get out of here."

Phyllis noticed blood on her slacks, once she was inside the car. Her lips tightened with resignation.

"Mitch?"

"Yeah?"

"I think you better take me back to the hospital."

"You're kidding!"

"No."

"All right, but the doc isn't going to be happy. You were supposed to rest."

"Yeah, I know."

"You've got a big 'I told you so' coming."

"No doubt."

TWENTY

THE SCIENTIST

All his life, Graham Gresham had been handled very carefully. His wealthy father, with his political and business connections, had seen to it that his brilliant son had the finest schooling and was rewarded with regal positions afterward. His loyal mother had seen that his epicurean desires were strictly adhered to, and his clothing was all from the best tailors.

But it was his brother Peter who had had the toughest job. Their parents had basically turned Peter into a janitor, mopping up after each subsequent mess Graham managed to get himself into. And he got into plenty.

There were the instances at university when Graham was nearly charged with rape. Willing coeds turned shrill when pressed for explanations from angry parents and university officials. Peter was able to pluck him from those fires with astonishing dexterity and, of course, their father's money.

But this last romantic interlude had turned into a first-rate nightmare of colossal proportions. He'd generally been able to sweet-talk his lovers until the knives came out. The women inevitably wanted much more than Graham was able to deliver and things got sticky at that point. And of course, that's when Graham called Peter to help him out.

Sarah Hawkins was a gorgeous beauty that Graham had his eye on ever since coming to America. They had crossed paths twice at commission dinners and parties, and he knew her father—Professor Harold Hawkins of Harvard University. Professor Hawkins had made a name and career out of atomic research. He had parlayed that shining reputation into several lucrative positions in the scientific community. The jewel in the crown was his position in the Manhattan Project at Los Alamos in New Mexico working alongside such luminaries as Robert Oppenheimer, Glenn Seaborg and Klaus Fuchs. It had been the high point in many careers during that time.

Klaus Fuchs, in particular, had been interested in Graham's career and set up a personal meeting between Sarah Hawkins and Graham Gresham. But Sarah had been a young woman with extraordinarily expensive tastes in food, clothing and jewelry, and Graham thought her out of his league. It was to his surprise and delight when Miss Hawkins had called him the next day for a dinner date that evening. His salary was quite sufficient for him, but not for darling Sarah, who soon came to be both lover and confidante. She wanted more than he was able to give and Graham was about to break it off when she sprang the news that she was pregnant. When she threatened to take the news public, which would have ruined him, or to her father, which would have been worse for him in the scientific community, he felt blocked in every direction. With dwindling resources and no way out, Sarah came to him with the idea of passing atomic information on to the Soviets. He could make a great deal of money and Klaus Fuchs would be able to help him.

Help him? At first, the idea was preposterous to Graham, not that he was a patriot. Those scientists with leftist leanings had always appealed to him, though he remained largely apolitical. Politics just didn't interest him, only science and women had ever had his interest. But if he was going to hang onto Sarah, something had to be done.

So here he was, walking down a lonely street to make contact with his Soviet handler.

It was colder than cold outside. A rare overhead streetlight dimly illuminated the scene. Flakes of snow fell steadily making the glowing light dotted against a dark background. Enough snow had fallen on the sidewalks to cover whatever footsteps had been there before him. His boots made crunching noises as he walked, thanks to a light rain that had fallen the night before turning the snow to ice. The sound seemed to echo off the buildings he passed, eerily standing guard and watching him. There was no one around, yet he felt eyes staring at him from everywhere.

Watching.

Judging.

No respite.

Graham tugged at the sleeves of his wool coat, wishing he'd remembered his gloves. He'd hurried out the door after his call to Peter and forgot his warmer boots as well. He was paying for his forgetfulness now.

Suddenly he heard a foreign sound. Could be

another set of boots walking in the crunchy snow. He glanced back to see a dark figure walking his way. His contact?

For possibly the first time in his privileged life, Graham felt he had stepped over some invisible line. His actions could really ricochet this time and wound him deeply, maybe permanently. He quickened his steps, thinking maybe he would get past the danger and duck into the café up ahead. That's when another dark figure stepped out from an overhanging doorway right into Graham's path. They stood a few feet from one another.

"Dr. Gresham?"

For a moment, Graham was too surprised to answer. When he found his voice, his words were shaky.

"Yes, that's me. What do you want?"

"I believe we are meeting tonight." The figure behind Graham caught up, effectively boxing him in. "If you would follow me." The man strode toward the doorway from which he had come. "Doctor? If you please?"

The man behind Graham stepped closer. Graham felt he had no choice but to follow the first man. And with every step, sheer panic reverberated down his spine, joining the terror creeping into his heart. The area remained quiet except for the closing of the door behind him.

TWENTY-ONE

THE ESCAPE

Peter and Jennifer stepped off the plane in Washington, D.C. Once inside the terminal, Jennifer glanced around at the spacious yet sterile environment. Their area of the airport had several levels with hardly any color in sight. She saw the occasional small food distributor, but mostly she saw lines of people waiting to board planes or standing around waiting for loved ones to arrive. Soldiers were in abundance, as well as children running along the slick floors with their parents scolding them to walk.

Women wore long coats over equally long dresses. Hats and gloves were the order of the day and Jennifer felt underdressed without her one and only hat. Peter had hurried her so much when they were packing that she only had her wool coat and the new mittens that she had knitted herself. A hat would have helped keep her head warmer. The coat barely went around her now and the front opening let in unwelcome, chilly air. She tugged on the coat to close it more securely, but it was a losing battle.

"You should call Phyllis."

Peter stopped walking to grab Jennifer's arm. "You must be joking."

"Why would I be joking?"

"Because we just ran out on her."

"All the more reason to tell her why we did what we did."

Peter began walking again. "She's an agent with a mission. We're a job to her, that's all."

"She seemed nice, Peter."

"So what? It's probably part of her training to be whatever she needs to be to get the job done."

"Pretty cynical attitude."

He took her hand. She stopped walking.

"Keep walking, sweetheart. It's every man for himself. We've got to fade away into the sunset. They'll get Graham now that their sights are on him. They don't need me."

"I don't think that's right, Peter. Remember Phyllis told us how the case is being structured against your brother? It won't work without your testimony."

"And I can't testify if I'm not alive."

"Then wouldn't it be better if we had protection?"

She stopped in her tracks and tugged on his hand.

"Jennifer..."

"No, Peter. I think you're wrong this time. You know that I usually go along with whatever you think is right, but I don't think you're right this time."

"Honey."

"No, listen to me." She glanced around the busy airport. "There's a pay phone right over there. I want you to call Phyllis and tell her where we are."

"I'm not sure that's such a great idea."

"We need protection. We don't have any out in the open like this without someone knowing where we are."

"But— "

"And we're in Washington, D.C. This is where Phyllis was going to bring us anyway."

"Jennifer, I'm not going to do it."

"And I'm not going to leave this airport until you do."

He flashed her a smile. "Awful stubborn today, sweetheart."

She grinned sheepishly. "Maybe you're seeing the real Jennifer Gresham."

"Maybe. Okay, I'll call." He stuck a hand in his pocket and came up empty. "Got any change?"

She laughed at him and handed over several coins. "You may need more than a nickel. It is long distance."

As Peter made the call, Jennifer took stock of her surroundings.

One man made her instantly suspicious. His hat was pulled low and he kept a newspaper close to his face. All the while, his eyes tracked the room. When they fell on her, a shiver worked its way down Jennifer's spine. His expression wasn't friendly. She inched closer to Peter in the phone booth. Though it was hard, she tried not to look at the man again. It wasn't necessary anyway because she could feel his eyes upon her. Maybe he wasn't looking at her and then again, maybe he was.

She knocked on the phone booth door.

"Peter?"

He held up his hand and mouthed, "I'm on with her." With his back to his wife, Peter continued the conversation.

"Yes, Phyllis, it's me. Peter Gresham."

"Where are you?"

"I don't want to say just now."

"Peter, why did you run? I told you I had all the details sown up."

"Well, it didn't feel that way and I panicked, okay? It's not like I've done anything like this before." Peter stopped to take a deep breath. "I'm trying to stay strong for Jennifer and the baby, but it's tough."

"I know it is and that's where I come in. I can have you in Washington tomorrow."

"Okay."

"Okay, what?"

"We're in Washington. We flew here late last night."

"Why did you go there without me? You know that's where I was going to take you anyway."

"I wasn't thinking straight, okay? I wanted to get the first flight back to England as soon as I could."

"Where are you in Washington?"

"We're still at the airport. Jennifer made me call you."

"I'm glad she did. Listen, you may be under surveillance."

"Surveillance? By who?"

"Several parties are interested in you, Peter. Now, here's what you do—check into the Downtown Motel on Seventh Street as soon as you can. That way, Jennifer can get some rest and you won't be in public. I'll get there as soon as humanly possible."

"Seventh Street?"

"Yes and hurry."

"Okay and Phyllis?"

"Yes?"

"Thanks for not being mad."

"Just keep off the streets and out of sight until I can find you."

"All right."

TWENTY-TWO

THE SET-UP

George Martin wasn't having a good day. His secretary was being promoted out from under him and he wondered briefly if she was sleeping with some higher up guy to get the new job at the agency.

He squinted around his messy office. Papers strewn everywhere didn't make for a tight ship, but he had lost control of his division some time ago. Possibly when Phyllis Schneider came aboard. His thoughts darkened as he thought of her.

Attractive woman with great credentials and a husband who had been MI5—that was the office scuttlebutt. Now working at the agency, Joe Schneider commanded the kind of respect Martin longed for, but never quite attained. That Schneider was relatively new and had a higher security clearance rankled.

Maybe he should have handled things differently. Perhaps if he'd been nicer to Phyllis, nicer to his staff, he'd be promoted now instead of his slimy secretary. He glanced out his door to see her packing up personal belongings to move to a higher floor, one with more responsibilities and more money. Martin had heard that she would be working for one of the career analysts whose star was on the rise. Dammit! She was chatting with people who came up to her desk to congratulate her. His congratulations were short with words he had to push out of his mouth, sour words that cost him to speak. She was too happy to notice that he was seething with resentment.

Nothing had gone the way he thought it would when George Martin started working for the government. In fact, he had been recruited in college, but he never seemed to fit, right from the start.

He'd made the correct motions, went to the correct parties and glad-handed the right people. Or so he thought.

But his evaluations always came up short for promotion and here he was, fifteen years later, working in the newly formed Central Intelligence Agency but not really much better off than when he started. To add insult to injury, he was being transferred to the weather division. Weather! What the hell would he do there? He knew it was a nowhere position in the agency.

Looking at his lucky secretary and thinking about bothersome Phyllis made him realize that you needed to be a woman to get ahead here. This wasn't what he signed up for at all.

Opening his desk drawer, Martin pulled out an envelope. Inside was a note he'd found on his car in the parking last night. The message conveyed was a meeting with an interested party at a public park not far from where he worked. The message said it would be worth his while to show up, but if he didn't, no hard feelings.

The message was short and sweet. Maybe someone appreciated his work after all. Since he worked for the CIA, it didn't bother him how the message had come to him. Just the fact that someone cared about him and was possibly interested in his career meant the world.

Glancing at the clock, Martin saw it was close to noon. He tucked the note in his pocket, rose to pluck his hat and coat off the coat rack. He nodded to his busy secretary, she was much too busy to care where he was going, and took off for the park. Her promotion and his demotion pushed him to the edge. Martin stepped onto the elevator with a spring in his step and a lighter heart. Things were going to get better for him—he just knew it.

Meanwhile, Major Dick Simpson was reading an advised report that had landed in his inbox this morning. He buzzed Col. Tom Metcalf in his office.

"Tom? You busy?"

Metcalf chuckled. "I'm always busy, Dick. What's up?"

"If you could come to my office, I'd appreciate it."

"Now?"

"Are you in a meeting?"

"Nope. I'll see you in a few."

Fifteen minutes later, Metcalf looked up from the report in his hands.

"You just got this today?"

"It was in my inbox when I arrived this morning."

"How could the polygraph people miss this? It stands out like a sore thumb."

"I know. I was wondering about that myself. Maybe they need to go in for a refresher course."

Tom looked down at the report. "It says here that George Martin didn't take the polygraph."

"Yeah, I got that loud and clear."

"Have you called Martin again?"

"Not yet. I wanted to go over implications with you."

"Well, the most glaring implication is that he must have something to hide." Metcalf shook his head. "I never trusted that guy anyway."

"I went over his last evaluation and, not only is his work not satisfactory, but he's gotten several complaints from the people in his department about a bad temper, mostly from women."

"What else?"

"He's complained to a few people about his lack of promotion."

Metcalf tossed the report on Simpson's desk. Dick stared at it for a moment before speaking. He ran a hand through salt and pepper hair in need of a trim.

"If he didn't take the polygraph, and I required everyone working on this project to do so, it means he didn't want to. I think George Martin has been doing extracurricular activities that he doesn't want known."

"You think he's the leak?"

"Sure looks possible. Since the old bookseller was a dead end, literally, this could be our next clue." He pressed a button on his intercom to his secretary. "Sally, could you ask George Martin to come to my office?"

"Yes sir. When would you like him to report?"

"As soon as possible, please. Thanks, Sally."

Dick Simpson picked up a dart from his desk. He and Metcalf looked over at the dartboard posted on the office door.

"Find a replacement for Hitler?"

"Yeah. Find me a picture of George Martin."

"He could have flunked the polygraph like Ed Meriweather did. You know, personal problems."

Simpson aimed the dart. "It's unlikely that Sandra was having an affair with Martin as well as Meriweather."

"That's not what I meant."

A mean smile sneaked onto Simpson's face. "The polygraph caught one liar. Maybe it's caught another."

He threw the dart swiftly toward the target on the board. It landed straight on the bull's eye, dead center.

"Good shot, Dick."

"Thanks. Now let's find Martin."

TWENTY-THREE

COMING HOME

Phyllis and Mitch landed late that afternoon in Washington, DC. The airport was mobbed with people coming off planes or meeting their loved ones on arrival. Phyllis took off for baggage claim, grabbing her bag as soon as it came off the conveyor. She hurried to the exit with Mitch striding fast to keep up.

"What's the rush, Phyllis?"

She didn't bother to turn her head to answer him.

"You know what the rush is. Peter and Jennifer could be in danger. I've got to get to them before someone else does."

He beat her to the car rental counter only seconds before Phyllis got there. Unfortunately, the only car left in the lot was a small Chevy, looking as if it were on its last tank of gas. Its fenders were dented and one of the back doors was rusted shut.

"You're kidding!" exclaimed Mitch with one look at the wreck. "This was seriously all they had?"

"Beggars can't be choosers, Mitch. Keep grumbling and get in."

Phyllis opened the driver's door and slid in.

"And you're driving?"

"Like I said, it's my dime, so get yourself in. We have to go."

Before leaving the airport parking lot, Phyllis opened her purse for the compact she'd expressly put in for this mission. She smiled when she remembered that her boss from her posting in Norway, Major Ronald Lawrence, had given it to her. Flipping open the compact, a small mirror reflected her short brown hair. She smoothed back several strands before tilting the mirror to one side. Shielding it from Mitch, Phyllis read the safe house address on the mirror. The address was for someplace in Oak Ridge, Tennessee. She was in Washington now and needed a new address.

How to get one?

"What are you thinking about? You've been frowning since you got in. Can you tell me?"

She lowered her voice. "I need someplace safe to take Peter and Jennifer once I've got them."

He lowered his voice like hers. "How about the agency? We've got keys and no one can get in there but staff."

Phyllis considered his idea. "That's not bad." She made her decision. "Let's do it. The building is relatively close to the motel."

Mitch held up a finger to his lips. "Shh. No more talking until we get there."

"You think the car could be bugged?"

"Who knows? Let's not take chances."

"Good call."

. . .

SHE HAD CALLED Peter from a pay phone by the car rental agency to let him know when she would be arriving to pick them up. She mentioned the make and model of the car she was driving and that she would come to the back of the motel.

It was dark by the time they reached the motel in downtown Washington. The old place wasn't showy or expensive, exactly the type that wouldn't attract attention. In fact, it was downright seedy and in need of extensive repair. And that was just the outside. She couldn't imagine how rundown it probably was on the interior and was mildly embarrassed that she'd asked them to check in there. Still, it was in a part of town with little street traffic. The motel itself didn't look as if it had many people checking in, so Phyllis was reassured that she had made the right decision on location.

Snow was falling so heavily when Phyllis and Mitch left the airport, that the town was disguised under a blanket of snow. If the circumstances hadn't been so dire, she might have seen a living Norman Rockwell painting with snow decorating rooftops and yards. As it was, few pleasant thoughts occupied her mind. She was too busy thinking about the next step.

As an agent, the job was always about the next step.

Mitch got in the back seat as soon as they arrived at the motel. It really was in terrible shape with paint peeling off the sides and chipped cement circling the building. Staring at the decrepit place, Phyllis Bowden's clammy hands slipped off the steering wheel. She felt warm liquid ooze from her body onto the seat. Oh, no! She was bleeding again! She couldn't think about that now.

The night was as still as could be until everything happened at once.

A black sedan squealed to a stop across the street. Three rough-looking men, secret police probably, got out and rushed in the front door of the motel at the same time her target and his pregnant wife stumbled onto the rickety fire escape on the third floor. Why hadn't she checked where the room was when she made the reservation? She had made a mistake that could turn costly if the couple couldn't get downstairs in time.

Phyllis held her breath, watching Peter help Jennifer from one landing to another, rushing the best he could. The third-floor landing shivered with the unexpected weight. The second-floor landing swayed precariously, making Phyllis light-headed with breathless anticipation. She was able to suck in some air when he maneuvered her to the ground level. Phyllis inched the car along the icy street, narrowly missing another car trying to pass her. A horn blared unwanted attention and she hissed a curse. She had waited for a half hour on this deserted street, only to have it become popular when she didn't need it to be.

Never mind. The situation was what it was.

Much was riding on this defection. If she couldn't bring in the target, his life and his wife's, plus that of their unborn child, would be worth nothing. They could be shot or worse.

Her job was at stake. Even though higher-ups on the food chain had chosen her for this assignment, she was still trying to prove herself to a boss who didn't think much of her abilities as an agent.

Most important of all, the atomic spy they had been chasing would escape justice. This man was as elusive as he was dangerous. Phyllis was in charge of the mission and she knew if he slipped out of their net, he could disappear forever. The Russian encounter with Igor on the train insinuated that Graham Gresham was going down, one way or the other.

More liquid trickled down her leg. Phyllis held her breath in the hopes that her body wouldn't fail her now.

Parked at the curb by the old motel, Phyllis kept her focus on the two people slipping toward her. Their breaths were frosty in the chilly air. The man glanced at Phyllis. She read desperation and fear in his eyes. She could tell that Peter was doubtful this would work out, that much was obvious. If so, why had he pursued this course of action? No one had talked him into this, he'd come to them. Putting that aside, she knew she could do the job and bring them in safely. They were only minutes from her car.

Snow fell heavily, caking Peter and Jennifer's boots, making their movements sluggish. The landscape was saturated with sticky snow hindering every step they made.

Phyllis opened the passenger door the minute they reached her car. Mitch opened the door at the back.

"Get in. We've got to go." Glancing out the windshield, she saw men stepping onto the third-floor landing. Their dark looks took in the scene with a glance.

"Come on, honey. It's not far now," Peter told his wife.

Jennifer didn't bother responding. With hands caressing her bloated belly, she panted from exertion. It took Peter pushing and Phyllis pulling to heave poor Jennifer into the front passenger seat. Her heavy load nearly reached the dashboard of the tiny car. Peter closed the door and slipped into the back with Mitch.

"Let's get the hell out of here, Phyllis," said Mitch.

Phyllis pressed down hard on the accelerator and the car lurched forward.

Her car's tires left deep ruts in the snowy street. Slush covered the wiper blades rendering her vision bleary. No matter. Weaving around slower traffic, she kept her car pointed north. North to the CIA building. Because of her precious cargo, she pushed the small car faster than she should have. A pedestrian appeared out of nowhere, walking into her hazy line of sight.

She stomped on the brakes. Jennifer braced her hands against the dash to prevent being thrown forward. Phyllis automatically threw a hand over to protect her.

"You okay?" she asked.

"Fine," Jennifer puffed. "Just keep going."

More liquid ran down Phyllis' leg, causing her to groan aloud.

"Are you okay?" Jennifer glanced over at Phyllis.

With tight lips, Phyllis managed to say, "Yes."

Heading out of the seedy part of town, traffic picked up. Recklessly, Phyllis careened her car forward with little regard for speed limits. With an eye on her rearview mirror, she could see two black sedans weaving around cars trying to catch up. Two? Where had the other car come from?

She cursed the rental agency for only having the one crummy car left in the lot, when she needed something that could accelerate faster. Also, she wasn't particularly smooth with the stick transmission and vainly wished she'd listened more to Joe's patient instructions.

Grinding another gear, Phyllis sped down the snow-slicked streets. Dim lighting from widely spaced streetlights, tall with small globes at the top, made for treacherous driving at best. At the speed she was going, safety was a moot point.

She ran a red light. It was that or deal with the dark figures in the equally dark vehicles tailing her. Incredibly, a traffic policeman was on the job, possibly because of the weather. He blew his shrill whistle noisily at her. Unable to stop Phyllis, the policeman was able to halt one black sedan from crossing after her. He pointed to the side of road, effectively taking one car out of the race.

By the time the second car was able to cross the intersection, Phyllis was well ahead, coming within sight of the CIA building. She kept her head down, both hands gripping the steering wheel with a death grip and her foot keeping the accelerator flat on the floor.

Suddenly, the car was veering from side to side wildly. It was all Phyllis could do to keep control of the vehicle. She'd heard a loud pop and feared the worst.

"We blew a tire," came from Mitch in the back.

"Yeah. Fabulous timing." Peter rubbed his hand on the window, trying to see out through the frosty haze.

"Pull over, Phyllis."

In a few moments, Phyllis had the car parked by the side of the road. Peter and Mitch were out in seconds, checking the tire and shaking their heads.

"We're going to have to hoof it, everyone." Mitch

opened the front passenger door and helped Jennifer from the car.

"Come on!" yelled Phyllis. "We've got a little time. We can make it!"

With Mitch and Peter assisting Jennifer on either side, the little group began walking as speedily as possible toward the CIA building. Phyllis knew if they got close enough, security would see them and come to their aid. They just had to get close enough.

PHYLLIS WALKED behind Peter and Mitch holding tightly onto Jennifer. Having to hurry wasn't something she could do well in her present condition, but she gamely pressed on.

Phyllis did the same. With an ache in her side, she clutched a gun in one hand and her left side with the other. She kept the gun close to her waist and turned back constantly to watch for uninvited guests. Just as if scripted, they were within yards of the Central Intelligence building when a black sedan caught up.

Brakes screeched behind Phyllis causing her to glance back for a quick look. Mitch looked over his shoulder at her.

"These the guys we've been expecting?"

"Probably. Keep going."

"Phyllis!" An accented voice called out to her. "You must remember me. Igor, from the train."

She murmured to her group. "Don't stop."

"Phyllis Bowden? It's me, Igor."

When she didn't respond, he tried again. "Phyllis? We need to talk."

"I remember you, Igor. Now if you'll excuse me, I'm very busy."

Footsteps quickened behind her. Clothing rustled noisily with the sound of several boots crunching hard in the packed snow. As more liquid trickled down Phyllis' leg, she knew her slacks had to be soaked by now, but there was nothing she could do about it. She fervently hoped that she wouldn't faint. It wasn't a good time for that either.

"Please stop, Phyllis and we'll have a nice chat."

"Can't do it, Igor, but thanks for stopping by."

"This isn't going to solve anything for our countries. You must know that."

"No, I don't know that."

"I must insist that you stop now, Phyllis."

She glanced back at him. He was pointing a gun at her.

"You see? Escape is impossible."

Mitch looked at Phyllis. He and Peter were half-carrying Jennifer, but both men had slowed their pace. His look carried the message of, "What do you want to do?"

She made her decision.

"I just don't see it that way, Igor." Phyllis turned to point her pistol at Igor. "And I'm not stopping."

Still moving forward, she nodded to Mitch, who quickened his steps. Straining her head, she saw guards at the security gate of the CIA had gotten curious about her little group. Phyllis pointed her gun in the air and fired off a shot. Everything moved into double time speed when the gunshot reverberated off buildings and echoed down the busy street.

The party of men behind her stopped dead in their tracks.

"You will be sorry about this, Phyllis," shouted Igor. "And you too, Mr. Gresham. You and your family will be hunted all your lives. You could have had protection with us."

Peter locked gazes with Phyllis.

"Is he right?"

"No, he's not, Peter. Keep going. We'll be safe soon." She nodded her head. "See the guards by the gate? That's the Central Intelligence building and the guards are coming this way to help us."

As she spoke the words, two uniformed guards with drawn guns reached them. Several more guards were heading their way.

"You're safe now, Peter and Jennifer."

When she heard the car start behind her, Phyllis glanced back. A smile and a hand wave from Igor, and the car turned around to return the way it had come. Phyllis exhaled her first real breath she'd taken in several minutes. It almost made her lightheaded with relief.

One guard came up to her. "I'll take the weapon, miss."

"I'm Agent Schneider and my mission is to bring in these people. Could you please call Major Dick Simpson?"

While the small group paused, the guard got out his walky-talky. Speaking quietly, he finished and put it away.

"You're cleared." He nodded at the second guard by Peter and Jennifer. "You're all cleared. Let's get you inside."

Within fifteen minutes, Jennifer was resting on a couch in an office in the CIA building with Peter watching her, obviously relieved. Perspiration beaded on his damp forehead, but his smile told another story.

Phyllis called upstairs and reached Simpson. He was exiting an elevator within minutes.

"So, Phyllis Bowden." He grinned at her. "You brought 'em in alive."

"As you requested, sir."

"Damn proud of you, Agent Schneider."

Dick turned to several guards. "See that these people go to my office and stay with them. I'll be right up."

After Peter and Jennifer were in the elevator, Dick smiled broadly.

"Was it a good idea to send Mitch?" he asked.

Phyllis smiled in response. "It was, sir. He wasn't any problem whatsoever."

Mitch's face reddened. "Well, I was just doing my job, ma'am." Glancing down at her slacks, he touched her arm. "Don't you need some help too?"

Simpson's gaze followed Mitch's. "What in the world happened, Phyllis? Were you shot?" He turned to a guard. "Get a car."

"It's a long story, sir."

"Maybe you can tell me on the way to the hospital."

She blinked her eyes in surprise. "You're coming with me?"

"On second thought, I can't. But Lorraine told me some news that I want to verify with you first chance I get. I just hope what's happening to you isn't what I think it is."

He spoke to Mitch. "Call Joe and tell him where you and Phyllis going. Ask him to meet you there."

"Yes sir."

After Mitch left to make the call, Dick took Phyllis' arm to escort her outside to a waiting car.

"I think you've had quite an adventure, Agent Schneider."

"I have indeed, sir. I have indeed."

"Come back to the office as soon as you can. I'll be waiting for your report."

TWENTY-FOUR

THE BOSS

George Martin had waited on a park bench in the freezingcold for over an hour. He looked as forlorn as he felt. Was this someone's idea of a joke? Well, he wasn't laughing. He also knew from training that staying in one place too long wasn't good for his long-term health. He needed to get out of there before he was seen and questioned.

Right on cue, he noticed a uniformed police officer walking his way. Martin rose to leave as casually as he could. He turned up the collar of his wool coat and turned his face away from the approaching officer.

"Hold on a minute, if you please," called out the policeman.

Martin quickened his pace, hard to do with the falling snow, which made walking difficult on the slick sidewalk.

"Excuse me, sir!"

Not slowing a bit, Martin twisted his head to address him. "What can I do for you, officer?"

"You can stop where you are, for starters."

Martin slowed his steps before coming to a complete stop. He looked back as the man caught up with him.

"What do you want? I wasn't doing anything."

"You can tell me why you've been sitting on a park bench in the freezing snow." The officer glanced at Martin's clothing. "You don't look like someone who would be sitting in a park for no reason whatsoever. I'd say you have a reason to be here and I'd like to know what it is."

George Martin bristled. He wasn't used to being spoken to like this.

"I beg your pardon?"

"Spill it, mister. What's your reason for being here?"

"I was thinking about life and minding my own business. Don't you have someone else to hassle instead of me?"

The cop's nostrils flared. "No, I don't. You're number one on my list of current interests."

"Well, I don't have to tell you anything."

"Yes, you do. I asked you a simple question: what are you doing here?"

Martin's lips tightened. "And I gave you a simple answer: I was just sitting. Is it illegal to sit in a public park now?" Martin turned to go. "I have to get back to work."

"Where do you work?"

"For the State Department."

"What division?"

"Apple Imports."

The officer cocked his head. "You know something, mister?"

"What's that?"

"I don't believe a word you're saying."

"I guess that's your problem."

"No, sir. It's yours. I'm going to take you down to the station for further questioning. I don't like your answers."

Martin was getting as steamed as the officer. "And I don't like being questioned for doing nothing." He began walking away.

"Stop where you are."

"No way."

He heard metallic clinking behind him and realized the officer had pulled out his handcuffs.

"I said stop."

Martin knew he'd pushed the cop too far. This wasn't going well and he needed to get back to work. This whole day had been a disaster, starting in the morning when he cut his chin shaving. All downhill. He stopped and heaved a heavy sigh.

"Turn around, sir, with your hands behind you."

"That's not necessary. I'll come along quietly if you insist."

"I insist that you put your hands behind you."

"Okay, okay."

After George Martin was handcuffed and led down to the corner precinct, he finally knew he'd stepped into a big pile of trouble. This was going to get back to his boss at the CIA fast. Who had sent that note and why?

In his office, Dick Simpson picked up his phone and listened for a few minutes.

"Is that right, sergeant? I'll have someone pick him up immediately. Thanks for calling."

Tom Metcalf looked up from the report he was reading.

"What's up?"

"You're not going to believe this."

"Try me."

"George Martin was arrested in Rose Park for harassing a police officer."

Metcalf's mouth dropped open. "You serious?"

"Just got the call."

"What was the idiot doing there?"

Simpson smirked. "I set him up."

"What? What did you do?"

"I wanted to see how strung out he might be. What I found out was how vulnerable he is to being recruited by a foreign entity."

"How did you manage that?"

"I stuck an unsigned note on his windshield yesterday. In the note, I asked him to meet me in Rose Park at noon today."

"Why?"

"To offer him a job."

"You didn't sign it?"

"No."

"So, the note could have come from anyone."

"And George fell for it hook, line and sinker." Dick shook his head, rubbed his chin. "What he should have done was bring the note to his immediate boss to have it checked out."

"He flunked the test."

"Indeed, he did. Go pick him up, Tom. Martin and I are going to have a little chat, right before I fire him."

"Will do."

TWENTY-FIVE

WASHINGTON

Phyllis was at wit's end. First, she put in a call to Joe, but he wasn't anywhere. He wasn't at home, he wasn't in the office, and his secretary couldn't find him.

Next up was a call to her sister to let Connie know she was back in town. All she got from her was a ration of crap about not keeping in communication better. Their father was in the hospital again and why wasn't Phyllis there to help out with him?

Actually, now that she was at the same hospital, she was going to visit her father as soon as the doctor, coming into the examining room with a huge frown on his face, was through lecturing her. She wasn't disappointed.

After her examination, the doctor gave it to her straight.

"Why didn't you get to a hospital immediately when you began hemorrhaging, Mrs. Schneider?" He helped her to sit up on the examining table, so she could see how thoroughly he was concerned.

"It...it just wasn't possible, doctor." Phyllis bit her lip. "I was in a difficult situation."

"You should have hightailed it out of wherever and gone straight to the nearest medical facility. This could have been so much worse. You were lucky."

"I'm sorry, doctor."

"Me too, Mrs. Schneider. I have to go back in to repeat the procedure that was done before in Tennessee. Your vitals are concerning me and the bleeding hasn't stopped."

"Um, okay."

"Is your husband here?"

Phyllis swallowed hard. "I can't get ahold of him."

"Very well. I'll have the nurse bring the permission forms immediately, so we can get you scheduled. This needs to be taken care of now."

After the doctor left, Phyllis lay back down on the examining table to wait for the nurse to arrive. She was able to breathe a deep sigh of relief that the mission was over and had been completed successfully. It felt good.

Once that was out of her system, she realized her physical condition was more serious than she thought. Would this new problem stop her from being able to have children at all? A new worry kicked in before she could get a handle on it. And, of course, at that moment, Joe Schneider walked in the room.

"Joe!" She struggled to sit up to greet him.

"Honey, lie back down. I met the doctor on the way in. He filled me in on what was happening, although Mitch told me the news in the car on the way over."

Phyllis' eyes filled. Tears slowly leaked down the sides of her face. Joe put his arms around her and pressed her to his chest.

"It's going to be okay."

"No, it isn't, Joe. I lost the baby!" she wailed. At last able to fully appreciate her circumstances, Phyllis let go and sobbed into Joe's white shirt. He let her cry until she was cried out.

"Phyllis, sweetheart." Joe pulled back to look in her tear-stained face. "The doctor said you should still be able to conceive. It's going to be all right, really it is."

She gulped back more tears. "He did? He said that to you? Why didn't he tell me?"

Joe smiled and pushed back the hair from her face. "He was probably too busy yelling at you for not getting to a hospital when you began bleeding. I guess you miscarried in Tennessee? Why didn't you call me?"

Phyllis didn't respond, but she didn't need to. Joe lowered his voice.

"You were knee deep in the mission by then, weren't you?"

She nodded, wiped her nose. "Do you have a hanky?"

Joe reached into his pocket to pull one out. He handed it to her.

"This is the one I gave you last Christmas."

"And it's my favorite, sweetie."

Phyllis blotted her nose. When the nurse arrived with the paperwork, she wiped her eyes as well.

"I better get this done."

"As soon as humanly possible." Joe turned to the nurse. "I'm her husband. Could I fill out the paperwork while she's being prepped for surgery?"

"Yes, Mr. Schneider. Please take the forms to the nursing station. I'll need to tend to Mrs. Schneider. You'll be called when she's out of surgery."

Joe kissed his wife, smiled and winked at her.

"I'll be waiting. Come back to me soon, Mrs. Schneider."

DAYS LATER, when Phyllis was out of the hospital and in better shape, she went to see Peter and Jennifer Gresham. They were staying at another downtown hotel, much better than the first.

The streets in Washington were filled with slush turned gray from constant traffic. Pedestrians stepped carefully through the snowy waste, trying to maneuver the streets without falling or slipping. People walked by wearing various kinds of eccentric winter clothing. One man wore a furry hat with earflaps, but had neglected to attach them under his chin. The straps swung freely around his face, occasionally blocking his vision.

Several people used umbrellas to shield them from the falling snow. When a chilly breeze kicked up to make the day even colder, one umbrella broke free and blew happily down the street with its owner chasing after it.

Coats, hats and gloves were the order of the day and Phyllis was prepared. Joe had dropped her off at the corner and parked to wait for her. She had wanted to say goodbye to the Greshams and wish them luck for their future. Joe knew she had to do this on her own.

Nodding to the officer standing guard at the appointed door, Phyllis knocked once. Peter Gresham opened the door with a smile on his face.

"Phyllis! Please come in. Jennifer has been anxious to see you."

While Phyllis stepped into the room, Peter went

into the bedroom area of their small suite. Glancing around, she saw half-filled suitcases on the bed. When Jennifer walked into the room, Phyllis met her to take her hands.

"How are you, Jennifer? This has been quite an ordeal for you, I'm sure."

Jennifer breathed deeply and smiled. "We're so happy to see you again, Phyllis." She waved a hand toward the bed. "As you can see, we're packing up what we have here."

"Where are you going?"

Peter stepped in closer to put his arm around his wife's waist. "We're going to Tennessee to pack up our belongings." He gazed into Jennifer's eyes. "Then we're traveling to London."

"To see your family?"

"Yes."

"How do you think that's going to go?"

"It might be difficult at first, but we're hoping my parents understand what I had to do."

"Have you spoken to them?"

"Yes." He nodded his head. "Father was chilly at first, but Mother took the phone and said we did what we had to do."

"Do you believe they've accepted what Graham did?"

"I think my father is having much trouble coming to grips with the fact that the son he loved best was a traitor to his country."

"But he's not blaming you?"

Peter chuckled. "I'm sure he is."

"And he married an American to boot!" added Jennifer. Peter tightened his hold on his wife.

"I'm so happy that I did."

"Well, maybe the arrival of a baby will smooth things over."

"I guess we'll see."

"Are you moving there permanently or will this just be a visit?"

Peter shrugged. "I don't know. I wouldn't mind moving back to England, but Jennifer and I will need to discuss it. In the meantime, we're putting most of our things in storage until we make a decision."

As they gazed lovingly at one another, Phyllis felt a tug on her heart.

"I need to ask you one last thing, Peter, if you don't mind."

"Ask away."

"Generally, I'm not allowed to talk to anyone about the mission, so I had to get special permission to be here."

"Okay." He cocked his head at her. "You want to know how the deposition went."

"I do." Phyllis threw up her hands. "I know I'm not supposed to and I'm way off base here, but this was a special mission for me in so many ways. I'm just hoping it was successful."

"I guess that depends on what you consider to be the definition of successful. I gave an oral accounting of the facts in this case; in essence, my brother was selling atomic secrets to the Russians. I wrote down what I said, with many details, and that seemed to satisfy those in the room with me."

"Will you need to do anything further?"

"Yes, I've been asked to come back for the trial."

"You'll have to testify at a trial against Graham?"

"Apparently so."

"How do you feel about that?"

"Not great, but in for a penny."

"You're getting pretty good at American idioms, Peter," Phyllis teased.

Peter smiled. "I said I would testify and that's just what I will do."

Jennifer took his hand in support.

"At least my good wife will be at my side."

"I hope all this won't hurt you in the future."

"You mean with a job?" asked Peter.

"Yes."

"Being an engineer, I can work in many places besides at atomic research facilities. I'm going to look in private companies around the London area first." He shot his wife an apologetic look. "I mean, that is, if we decide to stay there."

"Maybe out in the country," added Jennifer with a smile.

"The country?" asked Phyllis.

"It would be wonderful to have a house with a yard for the baby." Peter and Jennifer gazed lovingly at one another.

Phyllis had what she came for—satisfaction that her mission was successful for all the principals, save Graham Gresham. But his fate was on another path.

"That's really all I came for, except to wish you both the best of luck in the future and with the baby."

"Thank you, Phyllis," said Jennifer. "And good luck to you too."

Once she was back outside, Phyllis pulled her coat tightly around her for protection from the wind. She watched Joe staring out the windshield until he looked in her direction. The smile he beamed her way spoke volumes and made her feel content.

He leaned over to open her car door.

"Hi sweetheart."

Phyllis closed the door and turned to stroke his face. "What's that for?"

"Just for being you. I'm so happy to have you wait for me, Joe."

"I'll always wait for you, honey." He tipped up her chin to plant a

sweet kiss on her lips. "Where to now?"

"I need to check in with the office. Major Simpson wants to go over a few details."

"Sure. I can catch up on some work. Call me when you're done."

When he started the engine to drive to the Central Intelligence building, Phyllis realized what a lucky woman she was. A good job, a good man and a bright future. And with Joe Schneider by her side, she thought a few changes in their life might be called for. First, however, she had to see what Dick Simpson had to say.

PHYLLIS SAT in the visitor chair in Major Dick Simpson's office waiting for his return. His secretary had ushered her in saying that Dick would be right back. Make yourself at home.

She had never been in Simpson's office on her own and glanced around nervously, hoping he didn't catch her checking out his environment.

Very male, she determined. The Army had taught him to be neat and so the few papers on his desk were in a tidy pile. Several stacked folders awaited his return as well. His green wool officer's jacket was hung on the back of the chair pushed under the desk as if stated to do so in the Army manual. A stapler rested beside a can full of pencils and pens. Everything was where it should be.

But there were no personal photos of any kind. She knew he had been divorced so she hadn't expected a photo of a woman, but the room seemed oddly sterile without some kind of personal touch. Just when she was despairing of Major Simpson having any kind of jovial personality, she turned completely around in her chair. And there, on the back of the door, was a dartboard with three darts sticking into the face of Joseph Stalin!

The door opened as Phyllis sat quietly chuckling.

"What's so funny, Agent Schneider?" Dick Simpson strode into his office like a man on a mission. Phyllis coughed into her hand, trying to stop the flow of her laughter.

"Nothing, sir."

His eyes wandered to his closed door. "Like my picture of the enemy?"

"Seems appropriate, sir."

"I had Hitler up there for a while, but I needed a new target when he died and the war ended."

Phyllis smiled in response.

"So." Dick settled in his chair. He reached into a drawer to pull out a manila envelope.

"So?"

"How are you doing?"

"Fine, sir."

"I gather you had some trouble in Tennessee. Is it too personal to ask you about it?"

"What would you like to know, sir?"

"First thing, you could have mentioned that you were pregnant."

Phyllis lowered her eyes. "I...I didn't want to be removed from the mission, sir."

"You thought I'd take you off the job?"

"Yes, sir."

"Phyllis." He waited patiently until she was looking at him. "I know how much this mission meant to you. I never would have done that."

"Good to know."

"But I guess that part of your situation didn't end happily. Am I correct?"

"I lost the baby." Phyllis swallowed hard, pushed back a curl of brown hair that had plopped in her face.

"I can't tell you how sorry I am to hear it."

"It's okay now, sir."

"You sure? Do you need time off?"

She took a deep breath. "I think I need to do something, Major Simpson, but Joe and I haven't had time to talk about it. Finishing the last details of the mission, visiting with the Greshams before they leave and family issues have kept us quite busy."

"Family?"

"My father isn't well, sir."

"I'm sorry to hear that as well." He nodded at the folder in his hand. "But I'm not sorry about this."

"What is it?"

"I've placed a commendation in your file for the good work you did in Tennessee."

Her eyes brightened. "You did? Thank you, sir. That means a lot to me."

"You earned the praise, Phyllis. No one could have done better."

"I had problems, sir."

"There are always problems that creep up when an agent is in the field. How you deal with them shows character and training. You showed you have both, in spades."

A faint blush crept up her neck. She wasn't used to hearing praise from her boss. He handed her the folder.

"Inside that folder, you will see a nondescript certificate of appreciation with no names and no signatures."

She opened the folder and laughed.

"I didn't expect to see any."

"And you know I can't put my name on anything that could possibly go public. I don't expect you to put it in a frame to hang on the wall, I just wanted you to know how much we all valued your participation in this project."

"Thank you very much, Major Simpson." She set the folder on her lap.

"And I wanted to give you a report on your target and the subsequent inquiry."

"What's happened?"

"We've rounded up Graham Gresham, atomic scientist and spy extraordinaire, and he's currently on lockdown at a military facility. Of course, I can't say which one."

"Of course."

"His father has hired a top legal team to help him, but he's singing his little heart out to anyone within shouting distance. He's hoping to cut some sort of deal."

"Will he be able to?"

"That decision is out of my pay grade, Phyllis. I'm

sure he will be treated according to his crime. I would guess a few years prison time, for sure."

"Good. What about Peter and Jennifer?"

"They've been asked to come back for the inevitable trial, but Peter has already told me they may relocate in England."

"That's what he told me too."

"We will provide protection temporarily and British Intelligence will pick it up when they are over there."

"Sounds reasonable."

"I also wanted to mention George Martin's fate."

"His fate, sir? What about him? I assumed I would be working under him again when I returned to Washington."

"Nope. Not happening, Phyllis. Mr. Martin has decided to leave us."

"He's quitting the CIA?" Her eyes rounded like saucers. "That doesn't sound like him."

"Well, he had a little help."

Phyllis bit her lip to keep from smiling. "Is that so?"

"Yes," said Dick with determination. "With a little encouragement, he decided that his future did not lay with this organization. I will give him a letter of reference, commensurate to his position here, to help him with future employment."

"That's kind of you, sir."

"Due to the circumstances, it's very kind."

She didn't hide her smile this time.

Dick rose from his chair and walked around the desk to perch on the front by her. "I have one more piece of information for you, Phyllis."

"Okay."

"It won't make you happy and I'm sorry to have to be the one to tell you."

Phyllis straightened in her chair. She clutched the folder a little harder. "What is it, sir?"

"I understand you've been a friend of a bookseller named Mr. Leto. Is that correct?"

His question took her by surprise.

"Yes, I've been visiting his bookstore weekly at lunch since I was reassigned in Washington, DC."

"Have you enjoyed the store?"

She smiled. "It's a wonderful old place, sir. You should go see it sometime. Mr. Leto is knowledgeable about so many things. He always takes the time to talk to me personally and steer me towards books he thinks I would like. I'm pleased to say that he has become a good friend." She tilted her head. "Did Lorraine tell you I go to his store a lot?"

He nodded. "I confess I got that admission from her, but Phyllis."

"What, sir?"

"I have been to his old bookstore downtown."

"You have? Isn't it just full of great books?"

"I'm sure it is. I wasn't there to get a book and I didn't bother to look around."

Her brows furled with concern. "Then why were you there?"

He reached out to touch her arm. "It's a crime scene right now."

Phyllis' mouth dropped open. "I'm afraid you're going to tell me why."

"I have to."

"All right."

"You sure you're okay physically because this isn't good news."

"I'm fine, sir, just tell me."

"Mr. Leto is dead."

Her shoulders slumped and her eyes immediately filled. Dick reached into his pocket for a handkerchief.

"Here, please."

She took it to blot her eyes and wipe her nose. "Thank you, sir. Do you know what happened to him?"

"I do, Phyllis. He was murdered."

"Murdered?" She gulped more tears. "Oh no!"

"And I'm working on a theory right now that the person who did it was none other than your old pal, Igor, from the train. Remember him?"

"Indeed, I do. He also chased us down when we were bringing in the Greshams."

"He was, that's true. If he is the person responsible, and I'm pretty sure that he is, there's precious little we can do to bring him to justice. I just wanted you to be aware of what has happened."

"I appreciate that, sir."

"Your life has changed considerably since you accepted this mission, Agent Schneider."

"It has indeed."

"I hope for the better in some ways." Dick rose. "At any rate, you're to report back to the steno pool for the time being. Of course, you know not to speak of any mission business to anyone. I'm sorry to add Joe to that list."

"Of course."

"He probably guessed what was happening anyway." Dick smiled. "Didn't he?"

"He did, sir. Joe is a trained agent and is very good at his job."

Dick walked to the door to open it. "Farewell for now, Phyllis. We'll talk again soon."

"Yes, sir. Thank you."

Outside Major Simpson's door, many thoughts washed through her mind.

Mr. Leto.

What a nice old gentleman.

Her heart fluttered when her thoughts focused on a remembrance of being with Mr. Leto in his bookstore.

It was sunny spring day when the cherry blossoms were blooming all over Washington. People were happily walking their dogs and chatting in parks. She'd gone to the bookstore for a new book and to see Mr. Leto. His presence always brightened her day.

He was handing her an old book that had probably been on his shelves for years. She had wanted to buy a new thriller that had just been released, but he insisted that she read the classics. They would fill her head with thought provoking ideas and that was a much better idea than filling it with a trashy novel. She was going to argue with him until she caught him glancing at an old photo of a young girl on his worktable. The girl looked to be a teenager and was smiling happily at the photographer. When Mr. Leto had looked back at Phyllis, his eyes were filled with tears. She knew then that he was remembering someone he had lost. He pulled a crisp white handkerchief from his pocket to wipe his watering eyes.

"Allergies," he always said.

Such a nice man.

He was gone now. A cruel way to end his life. It

wasn't a far jump to know there was much more to Mr. Leto than he let on. She had seen personal mementoes tucked here and there around the store. He knew she saw them and it seemed that he wanted her to see them. Mr. Leto was gently letting her in on his personal life as much as he was able. He never explained about the mementoes and she never asked him.

And that was okay. Today she would take flowers down to the wonderful old shop to remember a man who was part ghost and part mentor to her. A man who probably had done a great deal in his long life, but was now at rest.

RIP Mr. Leto.

AT LUNCHTIME, she caught the bus over to the hospital. Actually, it was back to the hospital, since she'd only been discharged from there about a week ago. She hadn't remembered much about going in, but she sure counted the minutes until she was out.

Walking down various corridors until she reached her father's room reminded her of scenes she had no desire to revisit. The sterile, white environment with infrequent splashes of color was like her light-colored slacks stained with blood. Joe had thrown the slacks away and not only because they couldn't be cleaned. There was no way she would be able to wear them again. Not after what had happened to her and to her lost baby. Any time she saw them, she would be reminded of her miscarriage. The day after she had been discharged from the hospital, Joe threw them in the trash when she was asleep. He never mentioned it to her, but she knew what he had done.

Joe felt as bad about losing the baby as she did. Since it was so painful to speak of, they tried to communicate their feelings on other levels. Once, walking down a street, they passed a store selling baby clothes. Joe stopped to point out a pretty pink dress that a six-month-old might wear. Then he kissed her on the cheek before taking her hand to steer her away. He pretended not to notice the tears on the cheek he just kissed and she pretended not to notice his.

They also didn't discuss having another baby, but she felt certain that the time would come when they would.

Standing at the door of her father's room, she pushed away unpleasant memories and concentrated on the sight before her.

Connie sat on a chair by Del Bowden's bedside. Another man lay in a bed not far away, but Connie had pulled a curtain between the beds for a little privacy.

Her father appeared to be sleeping. Connie got right down to business. She motioned Phyllis outside the room and closed the door lightly behind her.

"How is he today?"

Connie shook her head. When she looked at her sister, Phyllis knew she had been crying.

"Not good. The doctor was just in."

"What did he say?"

"About the same as before. Time will tell."

"That's not much information, Connie."

"It's the best they'll give me, Phyllis. I've asked a hundred times how much time he has left and they won't tell me."

"Maybe because they truly don't know."

Connie shrugged. "Maybe." She fished a tissue

from her jacket pocket. "I'm not sure what to do." She gave her sister a big hug. "I'm so happy you're back in town. It's been awful trying to deal with this by myself."

"I'm sorry you had to."

Connie's eyes widened. She looked distraught. "Oh, forgive me, sis. You've had a terrible time yourself and I wasn't there to help you."

Phyllis sucked in a deep breath. "No one was there to help me, but that's behind me now."

"Is it?"

"As much as it can be." Phyllis wiped her eyes. "Let's talk about Dad."

"All right, sure."

"Can we bring him home or what does the doctor recommend?"

Connie shook her head. "We'll have to. He can't stay here. It's a trauma hospital and Dad is slowing declining, they call it."

"What should we do?"

"I had a good talk with a social worker yesterday. She told me about home care for him."

"Home care? What does that mean exactly?"

"He won't be receiving any more treatments, so we can bring him home. The problem is he needs care."

"Surely he can't go to his house."

"Well, he could, if we hire a home care nurse."

"Won't he need around the clock care?"

Connie nodded. "Yes, he will. Jeff suggested we bring him to our house because we have a spare room. We can get it set up for him and there will always be someone around to help him."

"You can't take that on all by yourself, Connie."

"And I don't mean to. I'm working part-time and

Jeff has a different schedule. The kids are old enough to help a little bit. They could talk to him, if nothing else."

"What about his care?"

"That's what the visiting nurse is for."

"What will be her duties?"

"As I understand it, she will monitor his vital signs and daily condition. His medication is basically for pain, at this point."

Phyllis grimaced at the thought.

"You can count on Joe and me. We will do whatever you need. Work us into the schedule."

"Okay." Connie opened the door and peeked in. "He's waking up. Let's talk to him for a while and meet back at my house afterward to discuss details."

"All right. Sounds good."

The sisters put on bright smiles to face their father. He wasn't awake for very long, but he was happy to see his daughters, and put on his own happy face. Later that evening, Phyllis and Connie made arrangements for what was surely coming in their father's life.

CONVERSATION WAS much livelier with her friend Lorraine. She and Henry had finally set the date, a seemingly impossible task. They met at Phyllis' usual lunch place, Walgreen's, with Flo, the waitress, in attendance. Flo's husband had sold a few vacuum cleaners this week, so she was in a good mood.

"Thanks, Flo."

"Any time you need a refill, hon, you just give me a holler." The waitress walked away with a smile to help another customer.

"She's in a good mood today," commented Lorraine. She gave her new hairdo a pat. "Like my hair?"

"Very trendy. See that in a magazine?" Phyllis poured cream in her coffee.

"I did. Claudette Colbert wore this very style in her latest movie."

"The one with Fred MacMurray?"

"Did you see it?"

"When would I have had the time? I've been busy."

"Busy doing what? I thought the Tennessee job was a walk in the park."

"Not quite."

Lorraine waved a hand. "Never mind. I don't want to talk about anything but the wedding."

Phyllis rolled her eyes. "Oh, please. Anything but that."

"No! Honestly! We've got the date set."

"Okay, I'll bite. When is it?"

"In two weeks." Lorraine proudly fluffed her pageboy.

"Two weeks? Are you kidding me?"

"Nope and it's going to be at the Jefferson Hotel."

Phyllis nearly slipped off the stool she was sitting on at the counter. Lorraine caught her just in time.

"I really am dreaming. Henry went for that?"

Lorraine's smile was sneaky. "He sure did."

"Did you threaten him or win a contest I'm not aware of?"

"Neither. My sweet daddy in Georgia came through with the money for the whole works!"

"Your father gave you the money?"

"He called Henry and wished him good luck. He said Henry was going to need it. Then he sent us a check!" Lorraine sighed. Her pretty blue eyes closed dreamily. "I always knew I had a wonderful daddy."

Phyllis laughed, drank another sip of her coffee. "That's great! Now if I can find a dress somewhere."

"Okay. Let's go to Woodies after work today." Woodward and Lothrop's was a beloved department store known for its ladies' clothing.

"Can't."

Flo served their sandwiches. "Eat up, ladies. Bernie only makes cheeseburgers on Tuesdays and they're going fast."

"Thanks, Flo." Phyllis lifted the bun to squirt on ketchup.

Lorraine smiled at the waitress. "She's sure happy today."

"Yeah, Kevin sold another vacuum cleaner."

"Anyway, Phyllis."

"Anyway?" She bit into her burger. "Bernie makes the best cheeseburgers."

"Phyllis! Pay attention." Lorraine snapped her fingers.

"Okay. What?"

"Why can't you go to Woodies after work today?"

"Oh, yeah." Phyllis reached for a paper napkin to wipe her mouth. "I got a call from Mr. Leto's attorney."

"And?"

"And he wants me to come by after work today. I'm already doing something, so I can't go to Woodies with you."

"Forget the dress," Lorraine insisted. Leaning over, she plucked Phyllis' burger from her hand and set it on the plate.

"Hey! I was eating that!"

"In a minute. Why are you going to see Mr. Leto's attorney?"

"He didn't say."

"And you didn't ask?" Lorraine's eyes opened wide.

"No."

"I would have pumped him for information."

"You would have wasted your breath. Attorneys don't talk unless they want to."

"Maybe."

"Oh, I bet you don't know."

Lorraine looked over at her friend. "What don't I know?"

"Mr. Leto is dead. Murdered."

Lorraine clutched Phyllis' arm. "No! How awful!"

"Yes, it is."

"Who told you?"

"Major Simpson. I really can't say any more about it."

Lorraine shivered. "That's fine. That old man always gave me the heebie jeebies."

Phyllis laughed. "Why would you say that? He was a sweet old guy and was so nice to me."

One brow lifted on Lorraine's face. "I have a theory about that too."

"Hurry up. My burger's getting cold."

"I think he sent you that note."

"What note?"

Lorraine elbowed Phyllis' side. "The one that fell out of the book that day on the bus."

Phyllis looked nonchalant. "Could be."

"I always thought there was more to the man than meets the eye. Well?"

"Well, what?"

"Aren't you the least bit curious about what the attorney wants?"

"Sure."

"Phyllis. You're not giving me much to go on here."

She laughed at her friend and salted the hamburger. "I have nothing to tell you, Lorraine." She patted Lorraine's hand. "You're just going to have to calm down and eat your burger before it gets cold."

"Phyl..."

"I'm very curious as to what the lawyer wants, but it won't do me any good to think about it. I've got a lot to do after lunch, so start eating."

Lorraine picked up her burger and frowned. Flo hurried over with a look of concern.

"Something wrong with the food, hon? That's one of Bernie's best burgers."

Lorraine sighed, cast a glance at her companion. "It's not the

food, Flo. It's the company."

"Can't do nothing about that, hon." She grinned at Phyllis. "Best eat your burger."

"Okay." When the waitress left, Lorraine examined her food. "All right. I'll eat this hamburger."

"Good. Let me eat in peace."

"On one condition."

"What's that?"

"You call me after the meeting with the lawyer and let me know what's going on. You know it's gonna kill me until I find out."

"Right after I tell Joe."

"Okay, I feel better." Lorraine smiled and took a huge bite out of Bernie's burger.

SHERMAN COXSON HAD the look of a distinguished city gentleman. He had a kind face, devoid of expression and accented by thick, bushy eyebrows. He was impeccably dressed in a navy blue suit that Phyllis knew cost more than a few months' salary. Hers, not his.

His starched white shirt contrasted with the dark blue of his suit and black bow tie tied smartly under his thick chin. With a few extra pounds showing, he'd obviously had a good life, or at least he'd been well fed. Sherman rose when she walked into his office, smiled broadly and extended his hand to her.

"Mrs. Schneider! How good of you to come so quickly."

"It was kind of you to ask."

He waved away her comment. "Please have a seat. You're probably surprised to be here and I don't want to lengthen your anxiety." He sat down and began looking through a pile of papers on his massive antique desk.

Phyllis glanced at the framed pictures on the wall behind him. Besides a law degree from the University of Chapel Hill in North Carolina, she recognized several prominent politicians in other pictures. In one photo, she saw Mr. Coxson with none other than Franklin Delano Roosevelt. They were both smiling at the fish they'd caught. Phyllis straightened in her chair. So, this man had been friends with both the president of the United States and Mr. Leto?

Perhaps Mr. Leto had breathed different air. He certainly had known interesting people in his life. She sat back wondering what in the world she was doing there. Sherman caught her glance.

"Oh! You see that shot of me with FDR? Lucky

catches for both of us. We had been fishing all day and just when we were packing to go, both our lines started dancing with the biggest fish you ever saw."

"The ones that got away?" she teased.

He laughed heartily. "As you can very well see for yourself, they did not get away." He put on a pair of round, silver-framed glasses. "Guess if I wore these things, I could find what I wanted faster." He held up a sheet of paper triumphantly. "Here it is!"

Phyllis stared at the paper held aloft. "What is it?"

Sherman Coxson sat back in his chair. "I've known Emile Leto for a good thirty years."

"Emile? He was French?"

"Originally from French Algiers. His father was in the import-export business until the first world war broke out. He and Emile worked in the Resistance for both wars. They were busy men."

Phyllis' eyes blinked wide. "He was in the French Resistance?"

Sherman smiled. "A true patriot was Emile Leto, but he paid a heavy price for his patriotism."

"What happened?"

"Germans burned down the houses in the town where he lived at the beginning of World War II. Local politics were rife with troublemakers, so it was said, and they wanted to make a bold statement so people wouldn't mess with them."

"What happened?"

"His family was lost in the fire. He tried to save them, but he lost his wife and a daughter." Sherman held up a picture, looked at it and then at Phyllis. "You have a real resemblance to his daughter. Here. Look."

He handed her the photo. It took Phyllis' breath

away when she looked at it. The young woman could have been her sister.

"Oh!"

"I know. It's interesting, no?"

She handed the picture back. "So that's why he always singled me out when I came into his bookstore."

"Probably. He was a sentimental old cuss and mentioned it to me one day when I had taken him to lunch on business."

"He mentioned knowing me?"

Sherman nodded, set the picture aside. "Which made more sense to me when he told me what he wanted done with his estate."

Phyllis quit breathing. She scooted as far back in her chair as possible and threw her hands out in defense. "I hope you're not saying what I think you're saying."

Mr. Coxson shrugged. "He had no family left, Mrs. Schneider, and he considered you like his adopted daughter."

She struggled for air. Beads of perspiration popped out on her forehead. Sherman handed her a box of tissues.

"Here. I keep these handy just for this purpose."

Phyllis took one, blotted her eyes and clutched it like a lifeline.

"May I proceed?"

She nodded and held tightly to the tissue.

"He came to the United States after World War II was over. Too many memories choked him in France and he wanted a fresh start. He'd made enough money as an architect to buy the bookstore, something he'd always wanted to do since he was such an avid reader."

"So, he..."

"He's left you the bookstore, Mrs. Schneider. There's an apartment on the second floor where he lived. All his possessions, his bank account and store were all left to you." When she didn't respond, he glanced over at her. "You need to breathe now."

Phyllis gulped in air like a trout on the line. "I...I... don't know what to say."

"Well, thanking him is out of the question." He smiled warmly. "Do you need some water?"

She shook her head. "Can you run this by me again? I think my hearing stopped after the first sentence."

Sherman laughed and picked up a paper to hand her. "Here. His possessions were itemized. His personal property is listed as well as the approximate value of the bookstore. Of course, the appraisal was done years ago and it's probably worth much more today. He also had some twenty thousand dollars in the bank."

"He left," she choked, "everything he had *to me*?"

"You were a good friend to him, Mrs. Schneider. He wasn't given to having many close relationships, after all that went on during the wars, but you made quite an impression on him." He looked her in the eye. "In other words, you mattered the most to him."

Phyllis swallowed noisily. "I had...no idea. No idea at all that he put that much value in our friendship. I just knew him as a nice man."

"He valued you more than you'll ever know, Mrs. Schneider. At first, I thought to talk him out of it, but I had you checked out."

"You had me checked out? Like you hired a detective?"

"Yes, indeed." His smile grew across his face. "You don't really work for the State Department, do you?"

When she blushed, he laughed again. "Didn't think so and neither did Emile. Since he'd been in the Resistance, he knew a fellow soldier when he saw one."

She coughed into her tissue. "Of course, I have no idea what you're talking about, Mr. Coxson."

"Of course, you don't and we'll leave it at that."

She stared at him. "Leave it? What do you mean?"

"I mean back to business. Here's the deed to his bookstore. The bank has been notified that you will be bringing the will and the death certificate by so you can close the account." He handed her several sheets of paper.

"This is all too much, Mr. Coxson."

"Perhaps so, perhaps not, but these are the final wishes for Emile Leto."

"It's going to take some time to process this."

"Please discuss it with your husband and if you both want to come back, I will go over everything once more."

After Phyllis left the attorney's office, she stopped at the bathroom down the hall before leaving the building. Standing in front of the mirror above a sink, her reflection was not the same woman who arrived thirty minutes earlier.

Her cheeks were mottled pink and her brown eyes watered for no apparent reason. Her curly hair looked droopy and she'd bitten off her lipstick. Reaching into her purse for her tube, the papers Sherman had given her fell on the floor. Picking them up, her watery eyes overflowed. For a minute or two, she couldn't read the documents in her hand. When she glanced back into the mirror, the filmy reflection was Emile Leto, not Phyllis Schneider. He smiled at her, visually approving her with a slight nod. Before she could speak, he faded until her own reflection alone stared back at her.

Knowing if she spoke aloud, she'd burst into tears, so she acknowledged him in her mind instead. *Thank you, Mr. Leto. You've given me a gift I can never repay. I won't let you down.*

A tiny idea was born at that moment and Phyllis smiled brightly.

"I have to talk to Joe," she whispered aloud. She could feel Mr. Leto nodding again. She didn't have to see him this time, but she knew what he wanted her to do.

After tucking the papers back in her purse, Phyllis blew her nose and tossed the tissue in the trash. She strode out happily and knew her future was about to change.

TWENTY-SIX

CHANGES

That night at dinner, Phyllis couldn't stop smiling. She'd put the dishes in the sink and had come back with several documents in her hand.

"I really can't wait any longer, Phyllis." Joe pushed in her chair when she sat down. "Come on, give already. Your face has to be tired from all the smiling."

"I have a lot to be happy about, Joe Schneider." She leaned over to stroke his cheek and kiss him. "You're not going to believe this."

"Tell me." His eyes locked with hers. "Should I be nervous? I know you went to an attorney's office today."

"No, you shouldn't be nervous." She paused. "I need to start at the beginning."

"A logical place," he teased.

"Do you remember Mr. Leto?"

"The old guy at your favorite bookstore? Sure, what gives?"

"He died, Joe. Major Simpson said he was murdered."

"Murdered?"

"Yes. I'm going to tell you a few secrets and then..."

"You'll have to kill me."

She shook her head. "Don't joke, Joe. This is serious stuff."

"I know it is and if you don't want to tell me anything, you don't have to."

"True, but it's all part of the backstory you need to know."

"Okay."

"Mr. Leto was possibly murdered because he gave me a warning note before I left for Tennessee."

"Was he warning you of danger you might encounter there?"

She nodded. "Actually, he was warning me to get out of my assignment before I did it."

"That didn't happen."

"No, but I met a Russian agent named Igor on the train to Tennessee. He tried to recruit me."

Joe's lips parted in surprise. "No fooling? I bet Dick was pissed off at that."

"He was."

"Did this Igor stop you from achieving your goal? You don't need to tell me the mission, Phyllis."

"Igor tried to stop me just as I was concluding my mission. He wasn't successful, so my mission was completed and I did what I set out to do."

"Sufficiently nebulous, but I can read between the lines."

"Anyway, I'm not sure about the time table, but Mr. Leto was murdered in his bookstore one night before I returned. Dick thinks it was probably because of the warning he gave me."

"This Igor didn't appreciate his interference."

"Something like that."

"Is there more to this story?"

"Mr. Leto and I had a nice relationship. In his mind, we were like father and daughter. The attorney showed me a picture of his real daughter and we look quite alike."

"You look like his daughter?"

"Yes."

"What happened to her?"

"She was killed in a fire, along with her mother. Mr. Leto nearly died trying to save them."

"Wow! There was a lot more to Mr. Leto than you knew."

Phyllis handed a document to Joe. He took it, scanned it and looked up at her.

"What's this?"

"He left me his bookstore, Joe. In fact, he left me all his worldly belongings."

Joe blew out a breath. "You're serious?"

"Very."

"Here." She handed him another two documents. "Here's the will and death certificate."

"I can't really read right now, just tell me."

"He left me the bookstore, which has an apartment on the second floor, all his personal belongings and twenty thousand dollars."

Joe sipped a glass of water and choked. She waited until he stopped coughing.

"Okay?"

"Why...why would he leave it all to you?"

"According to Mr. Coxson, the attorney, I was like his adopted daughter."

"I repeat: wow! This takes your breath away. No wonder you've been smiling since I got home."

"I can't believe it myself, but I'm beginning to be thrilled and delighted."

"As soon as you scrape my surprised self off the ceiling, I'll be thrilled and delighted with you."

She wet her lips. "There's more."

"Just leave me on the ceiling. I don't know if I can take anymore."

Phyllis chuckled. "Joe Schneider. You just wait."

"For what?"

"I have a letter from him that I found among these documents. Mr. Coxson didn't mention it and I'm glad now that he didn't."

"Do you want to read it alone? I can..."

"Oh, no you don't. Anything that happens to me, happens to you, Joe Schneider, so you keep your butt in that chair."

Joe laughed. "So, you scraped me from the ceiling."

"Ready?"

"Please read it. I'm all ears."

Phyllis opened the envelope with shaky fingers. She pulled out the letter that didn't seem to want to stay in her hand. She dropped it and Joe picked it up for her. Handing it back, he nodded.

"Go on, honey. It's his final wishes."

Phyllis scanned the short note and began to read in a clear voice.

"*Dear Phyllis, I know you are wondering what was in my mind—giving you my bookstore—but you have to understand a few things about me.*

"*My wartime activities precluded me from taking*

care of my family. Due to my involvements, my town was burned down, my home with it. When I lost my family, I knew I would never marry again, but I missed my family so much. Those long-lost feelings bubbled up when I met you and your friendship has meant the world to me. I know you've seen the picture of my daughter on my desk. Take a closer look: the two of you could have been sisters.

"You're only reading this because I am gone. Please take over the bookstore. It is a good business, one that I think you and your husband would enjoy. I know about Joe's background as well as yours, and I'd say you're both ready to make a fresh start.

"Please accept what I offer, Phyllis. You are the brightest spot in my life and I want you to have it all. All my best, Emile Leto"

When Phyllis stopped reading, tears continued to roll down her cheeks. Joe handed her his hanky, which she accepted with a grateful nod.

"He wants us to run the bookstore now, Joe."

"I got that, loud and clear." He touched her hand. "Is that what you want to do?"

"We need to talk it over, but maybe what we need is change."

Joe was quiet, thinking things over.

"Do you disagree?"

He ran a hand through his brown hair, graying at the temples. "I haven't wanted to worry you, but I haven't been able to be on top of things at work."

"The battle fatigue?"

"It's partially the battle fatigue and partially that the job has no interest for me anymore. I've got a million memories that I'd just as soon forget. How about you? Are you satisfied with the agency?"

"I just accomplished what I have most wanted to do in a year: complete a mission and have it be successful. I feel I've achieved a major goal and now I'm ready to move on."

"Hmm." Joe smiled. "We seem to be coming together from different angles."

"I think so too, oh, but Joe! Could we run a bookstore?"

"With all we've done in our lives to date, a bookstore might be a piece of cake. Getting through the war was a major goal too."

They smiled at one another.

"Connie, Jeff and the kids are coming over tonight."

"About your father?"

"Yes and to touch base. You and I have been pretty busy lately."

"But not too busy to help with your dad." Joe frowned and took her hand. "The doctor had worse news yesterday, didn't he?"

She nodded, fresh tears gathering. "Everything happens at once, doesn't it?"

Joe smiled. "Wouldn't have it any other way."

TWENTY-SEVEN

A YEAR LATER

"Did you bring flowers?" Phyllis and Connie reached into the back seat of the car.

"Well, sure. I wanted to leave my own bouquet."

Phyllis nodded, smoothed the leaves of her daisies and roses.

"It's a year today."

"It is. Thanks for the idea of us coming over together."

"You're welcome. I thought it would be more meaningful this way."

They stood at the gravesite of their father, Del Bowden. He was buried in the city cemetery next to their mother, Constance Bowden.

"I brought flowers for Mom as well," said Phyllis.

"Me too," added Connie.

Both women quietly contemplated their losses for several minutes before placing the flowers in vases set on the tombstones.

Phyllis took out a tissue from her pocket.

"Seems like only yesterday that we were all

together as a family. Mom cooking dinner, Dad breezing in to wash up in the sink."

"Yeah, and the two of us arguing about whose turn it was to wash the dishes that night."

Phyllis smiled at her sister. "Or some other topic that had us arguing. There were many."

"Poor Mom and Dad, putting up with us ingrates."

"They loved us to death and you know it, sis."

Connie blinked back tears. "Indeed, I do." She repeated softly, "Indeed I do."

"Remember the time..." began Phyllis.

"Oh, no! Not one of your family stories. You never remember them correctly."

"Says who?"

"Me."

"Well, anyway, Dad wanted to buy that red and white sport Packard and—"

"Yes, I thought Mom was going to kill him!"

Phyllis glanced at her sister. "That's not how I remember it. She loved that car."

"See?" Connie beamed. "We never remember anything the same way."

They laughed and Phyllis stepped back. "I've got to go."

"Joe already at the store?"

"Yep. I have to help him out."

"See ya, sis. Love you."

They hugged a long moment. Phyllis kissed Connie's cheek.

"See you soon."

. . .

THE SUN HAD GONE DOWN when Phyllis parked outside the cozy corner bookstore. Walking in, she marveled at the colorful flowers in the pots placed around and the cheery atmosphere that greeted her. Slight scents of vanilla and lavender came to her, so she knew Joe had lit a few candles.

Lights illuminated walls of books on every wall and bookcases throughout the store. They'd made a few improvements with decorations and layout. She always told Mr. Leto that he needed to brighten the place up. One time he had asked her to help him with that chore. As Phyllis gazed around the happy place filled with books and customers, she was glad she had finally gotten around to helping him. She knew he would be pleased with what they had done to the place.

A newborn baby slept in a sturdy carriage close to the desk where Joe was helping a customer. He caught her eye and smiled as she walked toward him. Just as she reached the carriage, a small whimper filled the air. Joe nodded to her as she lifted the baby into her arms.

"Now, now, pretty baby. What's wrong?"

"She needs to be fed, honey," said Joe.

"Oh, what a beautiful baby," cooed Joe's customer. "What's her name?"

"This is Betty," answered Phyllis as she admired her baby. "Betty Constance Schneider."

"Will she be a bookseller when she grows up?"

Phyllis and Joe smiled at one another.

"She can be anything she chooses to be," said Joe. "Just like her mother."

ABOUT THE AUTHOR

SJ Slagle began her writing career as a language arts teacher. Her initial interest was children's stories, and she moved on to western romance, mysteries and historical fiction. She has published 24 novels, both independent and contract and contributes to guest blogs. Her first historical novel, *London Spies*, was awarded a B.R.A.G. Medallion in 2018. She was given the Silver Award with the International Independent Film Awards for her screenplay *Redemption*, and she conducts publishing symposiums in her area. *Oslo Spies* is second in her trilogy about a young woman in military intelligence. She lives and works in Reno, Nevada.

CPSIA information can be obtained
at www.ICGtesting.com
Printed in the USA
LVHW042121020222
710073LV00018B/1743

9 781685 490669